34 Bubblegums and Candies

On love, hope and other such delicacies

Srish

PUBLISHERS & D

SRISHTI PUBLISHERS & DISTRIBUTORS
N-16 C. R. Park
New Delhi 110 019
srishtipublishers@gmail.com

First published by Srishti Publishers & Distributors in 2008
Third impression, 2009
Copyright © Preeti Shenoy, 2008

ISBN 81-88575-68-2

Typeset in AGaramond 11pt. by Suresh Kumar Sharma at Srishti

Printed and bound in India

34 Bubblegums and Candies

On love, hope and other such delicacies

For my Dad — Love is always stronger than death.

For Atul, Purvi and Gia —the three candies in my life.

For Satish — who is sometimes a bubble gum, sometimes a candy.

Contents

Preface

It is only in fairytales that there are happy endings and the Hero always wins. Real life is rarely like that. It is mostly imperfect. There are times when some things happen that are so embarrassing that you wish you had the powers to escape like Houdini or you could change things with the flip of a switch like changing channels when you don't like a TV programme. No such luck. You just have to grin and bear it. But the good thing is that no matter what it is, it always ends. Just like candies that melt and fade and the bubblegum that you spit out when you are done with it.

When I mentioned the title of this book to a friend, he said, "Sounds interesting. Really interesting—but why Candies and Bubblegums?"

"Because, there are incidents that make you ponder and make you want to think and may be re-think. Like chewing a bubble gum. Then there are others, spiked with doses of humour that make you laugh and leave you a feel-good sensation. Just like eating a candy," I explained.

He liked that.

Most of the incidents described in this book happened to me, and some of them to my friends. You may even relate to some of the incidents yourself and see yourself in some of them!

They just demonstrate that no matter how bad a day you have had and no matter how hopeless the situation that you are in looks right now, things always change. Always. It is just a matter of time.

If you think you have had a bad day, just delve into the candy jar. And if you are in a mood to muse and ponder, help yourself to a bubblegum. I have collected 18 candies and 16 Bubblegums from my life, in this book. But, what is a candy to me might be a bubble gum to you. It is for you to decide which is what— and we all know how deceptive it can be. Just like those sweet colourful balls that seem like a candy but when you bite and chew, they surprisingly turn into a bubblegum. Or that Bubblegum which suddenly has sweetness oozing out from its centre again, just when you thought that the juicy bit was over.

Each morning when you open your eyes you are gifted 86,400 seconds to make a difference. And that by itself is worth celebrating!

Acknowledgements

Heartfelt Thanks to:

My husband Satish Shenoy who means the world to me.

Ajay Chauhan for being a rock, morale boosting, giving additional inputs and hand-holding—all this in between his very busy life.

K.S.Narayanan for the countless delicacies that he always surprises us with and also uncomplainingly reading and re-reading whatever I wrote.

Sathya Narayanan who enriches our lives by just being there, of course his bartending skills help too!

My brother Prem Kamath for being there always and who told me I was capable of so much more when I told him about my newspaper columns.

Cherissa Castellino who shares every joy and every sorrow of mine.

Bharathi Narayanan who is always willing to empathise.

Chandni Pai who is ever encouraging, ever enthusiastic about anything I do

Niall Young who calls me the star of India!

S.K.V Prabhu who rocks, inspires and proves that age does not matter.

Rohit Srivastwa who designed my website and educated me about many technical things—I spelt your name right!

Also a big thanks to my friends for being ever ready to listen to me ranting about anything and everything : Suman Jeetender, Sujata Vijaykumar, Jayashree Chinne, Naazneen Pansare, Madhumita Goswami, Gayathri Shenoy (Babbiakka), Priya.(all three Priyas in my life)

And to all my cousins who have given me many happy memories in the growing up years.

A special mention of my online friends

Bibin Das (Whose words were a constant reminder to write), Prashant Mallya (Who is always ready to carry out anything I ask him to do), Guto Carlos & Ravikumar (Who always tell me how much they enjoy reading what I write), Asha Dey (For her kindness), Prathibha Rajesh (For her encouraging words) Shruti Kannara (Who is always thoughtful, always caring) and Rahul Kumar (For the times that he was there when I needed him)

Thanks to my blog readers and other online friends too.(You know who you are!)

Special thanks to the whole team at Srishti ,my publishers, and my Editor Ms. Satjit Wadva for the encouragement, tips and suggestions.

And a Big, Enormous, and Extra large thanks to my mom from whom I inherit the ability to laugh at life.

K was there when I got married. It was no surprise that I had chosen to marry a man like K. My husband understood my special relationship with K, and if he was jealous, he never showed it. In fact, K and he became good friends and got on really well. K came and visited us when both our kids were born.

Life now took us in different directions. We were in different cities, yet most mornings, after my husband left for work, and after my kids went to school, the first thing I'd do was call K. K was such a positive individual. I've never heard him say one bad thing about ANYBODY the whole time that I have known him. K had an infectious laugh, and a vivacious spirit and just talking to him made me feel so much better.

When I moved to this city 5 months back, I wanted K to visit me. He agreed after a bit of persuasion and booked his plane tickets. I was so happy and imagined us having long talks, in my garden. I pictured K lying in my hammock, gazing at the stars. (I have fond memories of philosophical discussions with him, under the stars, during another time). I was counting the days left to see K, when I got a phone call saying K was dead. He had had a massive cardiac arrest. It was like a very bad nightmare coming true. It left me frozen. Numb. Speechless.

You see, K was not only my special friend, he was also my dad.

My special friend

Many of us have a friend who is more than just a friend. A relationship that cannot be defined or fitted into norms defined by society. A relationship that you treasure and which makes your life richer, more meaningful and happier. It sometimes cannot be named and fitted into a pre-conceived slot as the bond goes much deeper than the mere definition of it. I am no different.

Let me call him 'K' and not give you his name, for obvious and the not-so-obvious reasons. K has always been a part of my life ever since I can remember. Despite the vast age gap between us (he was so much older than me) we got on really well. The age difference between us never really bothered us. K looked so much younger than his age. He had the energy of a man half his age, and the maturity of a man twice his age! He was that rare, perfect combination. He was also amazingly fit, tall and handsome, with a very striking presence.

He was an excellent swimmer. He was the one who taught me how to swim, when I expressed a desire to learn. He would splash water really hard on me, with a swift repetitive movement of his hands and joined my delighted peals of laughter, when I got completely covered in a water jet, created by the sheer power of his hands. We were like children when we went to the beach. K could run really fast, and I would try to catch him, running as fast as my legs could carry me. I never succeeded. When I could go on no more, sweating and panting, I would stop and call out to him. He always laughed and said, "You have to try harder. Never give up!"

I loved him with all my heart. And I think he knew it too—but we never spoke about it. When I was a gawky teenager, trying to find my footing in life, K was there with gentle understanding. After all, he was a man, and here I was, dealing with only silly boys! He listened when I talked. Really listened. I could talk to him about almost anything except boyfriends. I think he knew exactly who I had crushes on.

K encouraged me always to reach my full potential. It is only because of his encouragement that I have several academic degrees today. He loved all my paintings, and even when others thought they were just mediocre, K would always say they were brilliant. I don't think he ever lied to me. He sincerely believed what he said because he could not even draw a straight line, let alone paint! And funnily enough, his belief helped me to become better—not only in academics, art or sports, but also as an individual.

K was already married when he came into my life. He adored his wife and I appreciated the way he took care of her. I hoped the guy I married would treat me the same way.

John Cena versus Daddy

"Mom, do you like John Cena?" asked my ten-year-old son.

A woman would have to be out of her mind to say she doesn't like John Cena. (No matter what they say 'Oh my God—John Cena—drool—Oh my God' summarizes most reactions!) In case you don't know, John Cena is a well known Wrestler in WWF, a very good looking guy, a hip-hop musician and an Actor.

"Hmmm... he is okay," I answered.

"Ma, how can you say he is okay? He is the best," exclaimed my son who is ten.

"Yeah ma, you should see him fight," piped in my six-year-old daughter.

"Do you both like him a lot?" I asked.

"Of course, Ma," they chimed.

"What if John Cena was your husband?" asked my son saucily.

"What if he was your father?" I countered. "Would you like it?"

My daughter was all ears in this interesting 'adult discussion' between her hero (Her older brother, not John Cena) and her other role model (her mom).

"Hmm...maybe I would like it," answered my son.

"Well, I wouldn't. Definitely not. Positively, certainly, undoubtedly, I would not. Can you imagine John Cena, helping me in the kitchen?" I replied

"Aah! That may be something he won't do," agreed my son

"And can you imagine me cooking for him? Do you know how MUCH he eats? I'd be only cooking and cooking," I added.

My daughter now got the hang of it.

"And, ma," she contributed, her eyes as big as saucers to emphasize what she was saying, "John Cena would never have time to help us with homework."

"Or take you to the park."

"If he played pretend wrestling with us, we would be dead!" (Observant input from my son)

"And he will only have time for his gym and his crunches." (Another little analyzed titbit from my daughter)

"So, we will stick to papa," I concluded.

Both agreed happily.

Meanwhile, my husband at work was blissfully unaware that he had been pitted against one of the best specimens of Alpha male on planet Earth.

When he came home that evening, the kids told him, "Papa, you are the best. You are better than John Cena!"

He smiled smugly, looked at me and said, "Of course. That is why your Mom married me, not him."

I just couldn't help bursting out into delighted chuckles of laughter.

Round one to the father of my kids.

In every relationship there are ups and downs. Ours has been no different. In the thirteen years we have been married we have had some great times. However, there have also been times when we have had fights so bad that I thought we would never patch up and just wanted to pack my bags, leave and never come back. In moments of anger I have accused him of all kinds of mean and nasty things, just as he has done to me. But I realize now that, if there is an underlying bond of deep love, no matter how terrible the misunderstanding, the relationship survives.

Despite the John Cenas of the world —or maybe because of them!

Please hug me — I'm just like you

In the city where I live there is a non-governmental organization, one among many in India that offers residential care and rehabilitation to HIV/AIDS affected destitute/orphaned children and women.

Its mission is to enable children and women living with HIV, to get a fair fighting chance to survive and overcome odds; to ensure their rights to food, clothing, health, shelter and education without social discrimination.

Easier said than done.

I know, because I spent an afternoon of my weekend there. With about 60 children, all of them HIV positive and many with full blown AIDS. Some, with just a few days to live.

It was a soul-stirring, heart-wrenching experience. It moved me and humbled me so completely I still haven't recovered. I don't think a lifetime is enough.

I went there as a volunteer, as a part of a team, from my Husband's company (which encourages employees to devote a part of their weekend to some kind of community service). There weren't many people who were willing to go and be with the children. May be, it is because even though we all know that touching someone with AIDS cannot spread it, we still have that mental fear and loathing.(Remember Tom Hanks in Philadelphia?)

Since I work with Children (I do workshops on thinking skills for children) and since they really needed people, I said I'd go. I went with two of my husband's colleagues, whom I was meeting for the first time. We were all a bit nervous. This was the first time that any of us, were doing anything like this. We had heard that these kids were totally abandoned by society and nobody visited them much. Therefore, when someone did, they would be hugging you and there would be a lot of physical display of affection. Both of them had never worked with kids. In comparison, I felt a bit better.

It was a 40 minute drive. We got talking. One of them tried to convince me to put my children into one of the expensive boarding schools (he had been to one) I heard him out. Patiently. And did not offer my views.

When I actually saw the 60 odd children, the first thing that struck me, was that I had been nervous, for no reason. They were just like a bunch of any other kids that I had handled. Then I saw their purple mouths. Most of them had a kind of tincture rubbed around their mouths. (I later learnt that it was to prevent infections) I taught them a little dance and a funny song. I talked to them, hugged them, listened to them and made them laugh.

After that, it was time for Art. They were to make pictures—anything that they felt like drawing. Many drew happy pictures. There were very few who knew their full names. (All these children are abandoned children of commercial sex workers.) The ones who knew their full names wrote it so proudly. Usually, most children relate to me and open up to me. But there was one child to whom I could not get through, no matter how hard I tried. I tried to make him laugh. He did not even smile. His picture was a scribble of just one colour. Black.

Later, we distributed gifts and chocolates. What struck me was that there was no grabbing or asking or pushing. The children were so polite. They took it and said "thank you". One could almost sense a calm acceptance in them, like the limited number of days many of them had. Two of them said that they wanted an extra one, not for themselves, but for their friends who were too sick to come for the session. I went inside and saw them. They were tucked into their beds. Beside them, were the sweet and the gift which we had earlier distributed. These children were really used to looking out for one another and looking after each other.

The afternoon turned into dusk and we bade our goodbyes. How trivial all our problems seemed compared to the ones these children faced everyday.

We came back in taciturn silence.

There was nothing to talk about.

It happened one night

Ninety eight percent of the time, my husband is sweet. Really sweet. Not the sticky-sweet like cheap candy-chocolates that adhere stubbornly to every crevice in your mouth , but genuine sweet like a Godiva chocolate whose taste lingers long after you have finished relishing it.

The rest two percent of the time, he watches Television.

Therefore I was gob smacked, when he kicked me one night. Yes, he did. No, I am not making it up. It wasn't when he was watching TV either.

I did not know what hit me. Literally. Because I was asleep at that time. One moment I was warm, cozily snuggled up in the quilt, dreaming that Batista was pitted against Shah Rukh in a six pack abs-contest, the first of its kind for men, the concept pioneered by yours truly, and the next moment, I was on the floor, wide awake, with a sensation of cold floor and a dull pain in my side.

"Fut the Wuk!" I yelled rudely, and sleep made a hasty exit from my eyes, like orange pips spat out in disgust.

I looked at my husband. (He was not watching TV) He still looked sweet. His eyes were closed, and he was asleep, and frowning.

I grabbed his blanket and yanked it out, having discovered through years of practice, that this is the quickest way to shake him awake.

It was his turn to be surprised.

"What?" he asked, still sweetly. It is really hard to make him lose his cool.

"You just kicked me and I fell off the bed," I answered.

There was stunned silence. He was as shocked as I had been. Then he apologized profusely and we both burst into laughter. Then he explained.

The organization which my husband had been working for, had come out with a scheme, where for a certain amount which would be deducted from your salary, you could upgrade your car. If you didn't want anything to be deducted, they would still give you a brand new car, but it would be a standard one, not a premium or a higher end model.

Every one upgraded.

He had been dreaming of his ex- boss. His ex-boss is one of those 'Devil wears Prada' types. He is pleased when you suck up to him, steals credit for your work and then gives you a lousy rating, no matter how hard you have worked. You can never please him.

His ex-boss chose not to pay and went in for a Maruti Suzuki Wagon R. My husband opted for a Hyundai Accent, a higher end model. This was the time when Accent was just launched in India, and owning one made heads turn.

When my husband drove to work, and parked beside his ex-boss's Wagon R, his ex-boss just couldn't bear it.

"I didn't know you were a Punjabi," he sarcastically told my husband, in a disguised sugarcoated voice. (My husband isn't one.)

"Why?" asked my husband, genuinely surprised.

"No—it is usually the Punjabis who show off and go for big flashy cars," he said.

Now, sweetness is not to be confused with sharpness and razor sharp wit. My husband has both and his repartees were one of the reasons why I had fallen in love with this man, many years ago. It quickly came to his aid.

In a deadpan voice he said, "No, I am not a Punjabi. There are three reasons why I have bought this car. One- I truly believe it is a great car. Two- I think you are young only once, and if you are able to afford and enjoy the good things, you should go for it. Three- unlike you, I do not intend retiring from this company and when I look for a job outside, I can factually say that my last company gave me an Accent, and therefore they will have to better that."

His ex-boss sank into his chair and began to look busy. He did not say a word.

The night he kicked me, he had just dreamt that he was at the beach, relaxing with all of us, when his ex-boss arrived there, in a rusty old car. When he saw all of us, he began throwing sand on our new car. My husband was livid, and had dreamt that he was kicking him hard, which explains how I landed up on the floor that night.

It has been about six years now. We both still laugh heartily when we reminisce about that night when he kicked me in his sleep. The laughter, even after all these years, is tinged with that undercurrent of supreme satisfaction that comes when you outsmart a really terrible boss.

Today we are older and hopefully wiser. We have realized that what car you drive does not really matter. There is always going to be somebody with a bigger and a better car. There are also going to be people who cannot afford to buy a car.

Just like there are going to be bosses who are rude, haughty and arrogant. One cannot change them. Trying to get the better of them will only be like, to use an old saying, wrestling with a pig. At the end of it you are both exhausted and filthy and the pig actually enjoys it.

We have learnt that it is best to be like the duck that goes with the flow. To float along the river effortlessly, enjoying the gentle flow of the water and to treat barbs and insults thrown at you, like the water that falls on a duck's back.

And as for that kick in the night— it was worth it!

Radiators and Drains

Maybe you have all heard of this one before or may be you haven't. But when I heard it for the first time it made a lot of sense to me. What am I talking about? Am talking about Radiators and Drains! Not the variety of heat exchangers designed to transfer thermal energy from one medium to another for the purpose of cooling and heating. Nor the one that is an exit point for waste water. No, I am talking about types of people.

I remember reading somewhere that you can classify people into 'radiators' and 'drains'.

Radiators fill you with energy. You feel happy to see them. You feel good talking to them. You look forward to interacting with them. They leave you feeling really good about yourself, and whenever you think of them, you look forward to meeting them next. They are fun to be with, positive, upbeat and full of life. They need not necessarily be your friends. They can range from the clerk at the post office to the courier delivery boy or the guy who delivers newspapers or the mail man or that co-worker whom you never got around talking to or that classmate who is more an acquaintance than a friend. The only parameter for people to be classified as radiators is that when you finish interacting with them, you feel happy, positive and recharged.

Drains, on the other hand, leave you feeling down. They may not say anything unpleasant but after talking to them you feel totally drained out. Your enthusiasm levels dip. You are vaguely dissatisfied but unable to put a reason to it. Drains might have talked very politely and pleasantly to you, but after interacting with them, you feel somewhat inadequate. You feel, as though, something has been taken away. Again, a friend or a relative might be a drain. Drains are not necessarily people whom you hate. They could be just anyone in your life who leaves you feeling inadequate in a way that cannot be described.

A friend said that drains could also be called emotional vampires. She said when she was younger it was a big problem for her because she always wanted to take care of people, make them feel better, help fix their problems, and it took her a while to realize that they really don't want help. They just wanted your undivided, constant attention and the only way they are going to feel better is after they bring you down to where they are.

Another friend took the analogy further. He said that he has also met Fridges (cold people who leave you chilled), Baths (people who are full and make you want to dive in and soak), and even chemical toilets (they're full of crap) and he also once knew someone who was a cross between a food processor and a waste disposal unit!

Yesterday, I was telling a friend that the older you grow in life you become more certain of what you want. I am very certain that I do not want to waste my time with the 'drains'. There are so many beautiful, positive and uplifting things in life. There is so much beauty, so much joy. Life is so short and so fleeting. It is entirely up to us to enjoy each moment. There will of course be moments when you feel sad, hopeless, and despondent and, as though, all is lost. When that happens, it is time to pick up the phone and call the best radiator you know.

A-ha moments

A newspaper article yesterday spoke about 'A-ha moments' –the moment which was a Eureka moment and where you overcame odds and celebrated victories. They spoke to several people who had several things to share—like a fashion designer who said that her A-ha moment was when she started practicing Nichiren Daishonin's Buddhist philosophy and a Socialite who said that her Aha moment was when she became Miss Delhi for the first time, and yet another holistic healer who said that her aha moment was when she noticed the sun line of a client dipping and she advised some Feng shui changes which saved her life. (Her client's not her own!)

As for me, I lead a life a little less flamboyant and a little more ordinary. But I do have my a-ha moments too. In fact, I have several. I just had one yesterday when I realized that I had forgotten to wear the chappals that I usually wear at home (yes, I'm a true Indian, 'Hawai chappals' would be a more apt term for them as every Indian knows) and my son forgot to put away his Lego blocks. It was an A-ha moment—to be precise it was an aaaaaaaaaaa—haaaaa moment. (Ever tried stepping on Lego blocks with bare feet? I'd strongly recommend that you don't. One can do without such a-ha moments.)

Two days back there was another A-ha moment when I discovered that potato wedges (the variety that needs to go into boiling oil straight from the freezer) can actually explode, sending tiny ripples of oil, zooming out of the frying pan, sizzling bits of your skin which is now beginning to resemble a teenager afflicted with acute acne, except that this one does not fade away with Clearasil or the pimple zapping concoctions that promise miracles and the coveted guy. (or a girl— whatever you prefer!)

When we were in bed the other day, husband and I and were slowly getting cozy after a nice romantic dinner with some great wine and great conversation, (we had put the kids to bed early too) I had another a-ha moment. "I just remembered," I told him, "Tomorrow is the last date to pay the electricity bill." And everyone knows the impact that those dreaded words can have. This was more of an a-HA moment—and the ha-ha that followed later could have been recorded as canned laughter for a particularly un-amusing comedy, hastily put together for upping the TRPs.

Another defining A-ha moment occurred when the maid did an AWOL. I ventured forth bravely armed with a bucket and a mop (how hard can it be after all—and I hate my floors to be dirty) to do the sweeping-mopping. It was truly an aaaa-aaaaa-haaa moment. Muscles that I didn't know existed even after torturous ab-crunching daily in the gym, made their appearance like a guest role that a movie star plays in his home production and for the rest of the day, I walked exactly the way Giant Robot used to walk in the live action series that used to be re-runs on Doordarshan (national television Channel in India), during our school days when it was in vogue to watch them.

Of course they are a-ha moments! Where you overcome odds and celebrate victories! What else can you call them?

Have you had any such candies (or should it be a bubblegum) lately?

The Uninvited visitor

Like most bloggers, I too think in terms of blog-posts. Any event that occurs in one's life immediately goes through an analysis as to whether it can be converted into an interesting blog post.

I had a guest the other day. He crept in uninvited. And the shameless fellow decided to surprise me, in my bathroom. He was waiting for me when I got in. Luckily, I spotted him, before turning on the shower! My first instinct was to SCREAM—really scream, because I had almost jumped out of my skin, by sheer shock. But I controlled my impulse and had a close look. "Hey," I thought, "This will look interesting on my blog!" Yes, even in that fully-shocked, half-dazed, adrenalin-pumping state, the first thing that occurred to me was my blog. And, I deny that I am addicted. Does any one know blogaholic anonymous—-not that I need help or anything—I mean, I do think of other things—like Niall's blog or Sue's blog—or Mr. Fab's blog or Tim's blog or Rayne's or Katherine's.

Anyway, to come back to the story, I clicked a few pictures. (And they haven't come out too well, which is pardonable considering the state I was in). And then decided to scream. It was mostly for effect and also to test if my husband knew that I continue to exist, even while he watches Television. Just because I'm quiet doesn't mean I am gone.

So I let out my best imitation of the scream I remember hearing in Psycho. He was upstairs in precisely 6 seconds. Satisfied and happy I pointed out the visitor to him. He took one look at him, shut the bathroom door and said, "Well, I am scared too," and he went back to watching TV! I swear I am not making this up. My two children are witness to this incident. After that I had to go and get the security guard from our complex, who felt very important, helping a damsel in distress. He came home, managed to cajole the visitor into a laundry basket, with a lid, and then transported him, away from my home, and released him. All this, in view of about 17 neighbourhood kids and a few adults! My psycho scream had even more effect than I had imagined! All these kids had gathered to watch the proceedings. They accompanied him on the great march to freedom and, watched in wonder as he opened the basket and released the garden lizard.

Now a different view of the same story—this time, the garden lizard's point of view.

I've always lived in the garden, and wondered what went on inside that tall structure. At nights, for a few hours, the place comes alive. There is music, there is screaming, (a woman's voice which keeps going on about something called homework), there are some lovely smells coming from inside and after a while, it all goes quiet and dark, and there is silence. I have been watching this for a few days now and I decided to explore.

I got in through a magical opening on the wall which is sometimes there and sometimes not there. (I later understood that this is what those humans refer to as windows.) There was a huge structure with something soft on it, and it didn't look too good to climb on. So I ventured further in. I was scared, but I wanted to see what lay ahead. There were no plants to hide behind, in case somebody came. There was this little white thing and it gave me some kind of a shelter. I decided to go behind it, and was just settling into a comfortable position when suddenly an enormous creature with two legs walked in. I think this is the female human whose voice I hear every night. Suddenly she points something strange at me, and it goes "flash", "flash" thrice. Then she vanishes. I am really scared now. But there is no opening, now. Like I told you, it appears and disappears at will. So I have to wait. I wait with my heart pounding and another human appears very briefly through the magical opening. Then he too vanishes almost as quickly as he appeared. By this time I am desperately looking for more places to hide. I wish there were some plants here. I wish I had never ventured in. All of a sudden there are lots of human voices. They sound like baby humans. I decide to keep quiet and scare them if they come near. But, wait —here is a new human—he has something in his hand.. He doesn't seem to be scared of me. Help! He has caught me now and I am inside a huge prison, with no way out. The prison is moving. I am moving wildly inside it. I am trapped and there is no escape. I am certain this is the last I'll see of my garden.

Suddenly the moving stops. The prison is open. I wait for a second and scamper to safety. I can see all the baby humans watching me. I

look around. It is going to take me a while to find my way back home—but at least I'm alive!

After that incident, I always double check before I have a bath. You never know what you might find in there apart from the bath water!

I have long since concluded that sometimes, when things do not go the way you want them to, when someone does not behave the way you expected them to or when someone unexpectedly turns up where they are not supposed to, it might momentarily shake you. But it always helps when you look at it from the other person's point of view.

Feeling Needed

We all like to be needed. Most of us, anyway. It gives us an ego-kick and a sense of importance. It makes us feel wanted and useful. It makes us feel that we matter.

Kids grow up and stop depending on parents after a certain age. Then they depend on their friends. It may not be wrong to say that after a while, it is the parents who need the kids more than the now grown-up adult children. The bond gets nurtured only by the efforts one puts in. The more one sows, the more one reaps.

Most seasoned parents (and by 'seasoned' I mean parents who have two kids or more who are older than five years—until then you are just a novice) swear that there are laws of Universe conspiring to make their progeny as different as possible from each other. If one likes pizzas and burgers, the other will usually prefer fresh vegetables and low calorie health food. (Yes, there are kids like that!) If one likes

Nirvana, the other will lik. Bollywood songs with rhythmic beats, and if one is a late bird, chance are the other will most probably be an early riser.

My daughter (who is now seven) is an early bird. To add to that she is an eager-beaver as well. Bright eyed, bushy tailed, up at the crack of dawn, (her chirpiness directly proportional to the earlier hour) she will usually go and bring a book and sit on my back (while I am sprawled on the bed, my back becoming a comfortable seat for her) and read aloud, because I have left strict instructions that if she wakes up earlier than me, she has to entertain herself unless the house is on fire—in which case she is allowed to wake me. I am a late bird and would have gone to bed only at 1:00 am—and 5:15 am is midnight for me. I have threatened her, cajoled her, begged her, pleaded with her and even tried sleeping with cotton stuffed in my ears—but to no avail.

"Maaaaaa…Maaaaaa!" she will go on, in a sweet honey coated voice (which in reality is delightful but at 5:15 am in the morning it is more saccharine, less sugar). "What is this word?" she will ask. "I am not waking you up maaa. I just want you to tell me one word. I am getting stuck, you see—and it is FIRST—ating."

No, thank you! I don't see and I don't want to see. So I mumble asking her to spell it. Usually the word would be one with an apostrophe or something that is hyphenated—and even a simple word like 'I'd' becomes ID when the apostrophe is not read out. So I'll mumble that I don't know what it is and plead with her to let me sleep for 10 more minutes.

At this point she will stick the book about 2 centimeters away from my eyes.

"Maaaa—just see once. If you tell me what it is just once, I promise I will let you sleep."

Deal sealed, I'll grudgingly open one eye and read out the word.

After precisely one and a half minutes, (just at that point when sleep is slowly descending on me like the sun setting on a clear day) she will say, "Maaa...Are 10 minutes over?"

I fixed that problem. At least I presumed I did. (But I had presumed wrong.)

I taught her how to measure how much a minute is. I taught her to say "One thousand one... One thousand two... One thousand three, and so on up to one thousand sixty." It would take approximately a minute. And for ten minutes she has to say it ten times. She understood perfectly and nodded delightedly at the new discovery.

These days, in addition to "Maaaa...What word is this?" I also have to listen to her shouting "One thousand one, one thousand two..." at the top of her voice at 5:15 am.

I asked her why she does not ever bother my husband. I asked why she does not wake *him* up for a change. Why does he get away scot free?

"Aww mummy," she said, "Papa will never wake up. You always tell me what I want to know. Look ma, if I knew how to read I would not bother you."

You can't argue with logic like that.

And secretly I do enjoy it while it lasts.

Like I said, it is nice to be needed —sometimes, even if it is at 5:15 in the morning. It is also good to remind oneself that even though it is nice to be needed, there is always a price to pay!

The two monsters

It was a pleasant and windy day. The children in the neighborhood were playing and I was on a park bench watching them. They were talking and discussing what they would become when they grew up. It was a serious discussion and they meant every word of it, with complete conviction and zero doubts. It made me think how different they are from adults. They are not afraid to imagine and they are not afraid to dream. They are not afraid to fall down and if they do, they just get up and carry on with life. It made me wonder as to why we adults do not have the enthusiasm that the children do, to try out new things. Why are we so enclosed in our comfort zones, not wanting to step out? May be it is because of the two monsters.

Inside most of us, live two monsters. Mr. YES and Mr. NO. You can call them Ms. YES and Ms. NO, if you prefer. Or just Y and N, to keep it really simple.

Y likes you. Y appreciates anything you do. When you look in the mirror Y says, "Yes, you look good. You aren't fat. You have not put on too much weight. Your complexion is looking clearer. You are smart. Yes, I like you. You are great, gorgeous, the best person in the world. I like hanging around with you and you make me happy. You are talented, smart and witty. The people in your life value you and you are important to them."

N is not so kind. N criticizes any thing you do. "You can be thinner. You look tired. What are those dark circles under your eyes? You are just average. I am not too fond of you. What you are doing is nothing great. You are just average. You are not important. You are foolish, silly and unattractive."

Y believes in you. Y thinks you can achieve anything. N tells you that your ideas are not good. N reminds you what it is to be ridiculed. Y sets you free. N holds you back.

N is sometimes useful, when it pushes you into doing something about whatever has been bothering you. Like ending a relationship with that constant cribber, the critic, the so-called friend who was actually not one. But if you let N take over completely, you get defeated.

Most psychologists agree that it is mostly because of N that many people find it difficult to accept or give praise. When you praise someone sincerely, instead of accepting it as a compliment and saying thank you, they dismiss it as flattery. It is like getting a gift for somebody and having it thrown back at your face. N simply does not let you believe that you are good. N does not let you believe in yourself or in others. Many people find it difficult to tell others that they really admire them, or something they did. You see, it is N at work. ("What will that person think? Will she/he think that I want something and so I am praising them? How will I sound?")

There is a constant battle going on inside between the starry-eyed affirmation and the disapproving-eyed negation.

When I was thinking of writing this book N tried to stop me. Actually N and many other people, in the voice of N tried. I am glad Y won.

If N perks up its head when you really want to pursue your dreams, it is best to tell N to buzz off. This simple philosophy has been propounded by many positive thinkers and is described in many books. Paulo Coelho, Rhonda Byrne, Robin Sharma, Shiv Khera, Norman Vincent Peale—all of them convey a similar underlying message.

They believe that people can shape their thoughts and use the laws of attraction to turn their lives around. What most of them say is that you should deeply and badly want it from the heart (not merely an unexpressed wishful thinking).

Powerful words indeed: "Believe and you shall achieve."

Sly Stallone does not open so easily!

Have you ever got a laughter attack? Laughed like a lunatic for absolutely no reason? And then, when you are in that mode, everything, every single little thing which is so ordinary seems really funny and you just can't stop laughing. It is a bit like being drunk except that you are completely sober and in your senses, but your rib has gone into auto tickling mode, just like a computer that has hung and you laugh and laugh and laugh.

A friend of mine and I have got into this mode a couple of times. She used to live in the apartment next to mine on the sixth floor. Hours after our kids and husbands left for school and work, we would stand on our respective balconies which were adjacent to each others, and we would talk over a leisurely cup of tea. Our apartment complex was located behind a group of posh office buildings that housed many software giants and multinationals and so it always had a crowd of young office goers hanging around, taking a break. My friend would pick the best looking guys of the lot and tell me, "He is yours and that one there is mine." I would see whom she picked for me and herself and we would giggle like silly school girls and not the supposedly responsible mothers of two that we were.

She rang my bell frantically one afternoon. The cooking gas cylinder in her house had just got over. If you have lived in India, you'll know what a big disaster that is. Most places in India use LPG cylinders and have not yet switched to piped gas. You would also probably know that sometimes it can be really hard to open that white plastic cap of a new cylinder, which is attached with a nylon string that can cut your hand if you aren't too careful or if you have tugged too hard.

I had a spare cylinder and between both of us, we managed to pant and heave and push it into her home. Then came part two. We tried opening it. We tugged and yanked at the nylon thread. The cap didn't budge. She tried again and then I did. We tried for at least fifteen minutes and gave up. It just wasn't budging. She needed to connect it as she was expecting her Mother-in-law and her husband's side of the family in the evening.

"Murphy's Law," I said

"Yes, and what an awful day for this to happen! It has to happen only today," she agreed.

We tried again and when we couldn't, we decided that we needed a man for the job. Since both our husbands were at work, we decided to go upstairs to the seventh floor. Seventh floor housed penthouses and many of the posh offices had their service apartments there. Who better to help us than the caretakers there? So we went up and asked the guy who opened the door whether he could help us.

Two ladies—damsels in distress asking for help. I think it would make most men feel macho and most men would help. This smart looking guy was no different and he came downstairs with us. We pointed out the cylinder and he began tugging at the string. He was trying really hard and his face contorted because of the effort. My friend then got a laughter attack seeing him struggle. She ran out of the kitchen and I could see her almost collapsing on the sofa, behind his back. I could see her stuffing a hanky over her mouth to stop. Laughter is really infectious and her crazy behavior was affecting me too. To my horror, I found myself trying to suppress my laughter while the poor man struggled and panted. I just couldn't hold it in anymore and I was so embarrassed as the guy would think we were laughing at him. (Which we actually were—and to top it my friend was pointing at his shapely butt which was outlined so well as he bent over—and that made me double up even more.) I said the first thing that came to my head. "This gas cylinder does not open up easily. It is like Sylvester Stallone." And we both burst out into loud raucous guffaws like it was the funniest thing on earth, so relieved that we could explode with laughter.

The guy looked at us with a dead pan expression. He did not even smile. He probably concluded that we were mad and said, "*Madam, humse nahin hoga .Mein apne Boss ko bulaoonga.*" (I am not able to do it. I shall ask my boss to help you.)

I managed to thank him.

I had threatened my friend with dire consequences (that included stopping all the tea-sipping chat sessions on the balcony) if she as much dared smile when the boss came. And after two minutes the Boss arrived to help us.

We again pointed out the offending cylinder. He bent over and tugged the string and at that moment there was a distinct sound that went 'prrrrrrrrrrrrrrrrrr.' Honestly I don't know if it was his trouser ripping or whether it was gas being let out. (And not from the cylinder either.) Exactly at the same time, the string gave way and the man stood up straight triumphantly—mission accomplished. It was enough to send us into the mad land of laughter. The Boss thought we were laughing in joy, and we managed to thank him for helping us.

The moment he went out, we rolled on the floor and I am sure he heard us. I promptly told her that he was *hers* (and not mine, I emphasized) as he had helped *her*.

I am certain in fact that they heard us that day, because after that day, both of them quickly look the other way if they run into us in the lobby or while waiting for the elevator or at the parking lot.

I have moved to a different place now, and when I call her up these days just asking her "How is *your* boss in the penthouse?" is enough to send us both into mad giggles.

You don't realize it when it is happening but sometimes, in life, it is these unexpected gifts like crazy laughing sessions with friends that you long cherish, even years after the moment has passed.

Have a nice day!

On a good day, there are more things (like story books, parts of toys, bits of craft material, colouring books, crayons, markers with caps off and caps with markers off) scattered across my bedroom floor, than landmines in a battlefield in WW II. On a bad day, let's just say I have an intense longing to have powers like Moses, who parted the sea.

On a good day, I organize a 'Lets-see-who-collects-the-maximum-things-in-one-minute' contest with enthusiastic participation, from husband and two kids, the prize being that the winner gets to sleep with me. (Husband wins on most good days— He says the prize is irresistible!)

On a bad day, I organize my vocal chords and yell. Real loud. It always works, the fringe benefit being that, since I am grumpy and in a bad mood, I get to sleep by myself, in the six-by-six bed. I simply love fringe benefits!

On a good day, I drag myself out of bed, after hitting the snooze button on the alarm clock, at least thrice trying ineptly to keep my eyes open, light the stove and make coffee all at the same time. On a bad day, the kids drag me out of bed with rhythmic chants of "Wake up Ma—we will be late. Wake up Ma—it's already eight."

On a good day, the kids have at least three serious fights in a span of forty five minutes, before getting ready for school, punctuated liberally with yells of "MOM—HE is killing me—Come quick!" to "MOM—SHE started it—She bit me first. If you don't do something, I'll call the Police."

On a bad day, it is the husband and I who fight. We don't yell – but the silent, cold war with hostilities cleverly disguised, gritted teeth, fake sweetness, dripping sarcasm and veiled digs cannot be missed.

On a good day, the tie and the identity card to be worn to school are found after a fifteen-minute search expedition that involves maid, granny and a hassled dad and even more harassed mom, searching frantically in all places, especially inside the washing machine.

On a bad day, it is found after a half-hour search and a forced confession extracted from one of the kids that they actually hid the other child's tie, after a fight referred to on a bad day. (On a really bad day, we find it *after* we have filled up a form and paid the fine at school for losing it.)

On a good day, I get to read the newspaper at 10:30 am, after everyone has left. On a bad day, I discover that the newspaper has been used to wrap a school project that has to be turned in, and I discover this after I have looked in every possible place that it could be, including under the mattress, just in case the kids remembered my yelling from the bad day.

On a good day, I always remind myself, there are days which can be worse. On a bad day, I am reminded what Charlene Ann Baumbich said, "Mama said there'd be days like this—but she didn't say how many!"

I'm thankful for the good days. I'm thankful for the bad days, too. It means that I am well and healthy. I don't have any serious ailments to worry about. I have a happy family and a cozy home. Besides, I can always have a great haircut on a bad day. My hairdresser tells me she styles it best, when it is standing up!

So, you see, it is all a matter of perspective and when people tell me, "Have a nice day!" I smile because I know either way I will!

Dance like no one is watching

The kids and I were bored. Not bored in a nothing-to-do sort of way, but bored in a everything-that-has-to-be-done-is-so-mundane-and-boring sort of way. Husband had just left for UK the previous night, and it was snowing in London. He was shivering there while we were getting roasted and fried, toasted and browned in the gorgeous start of what promised to be a very hot summer.

To alleviate the boredom a bit and mainly to kick-start and inject life into a lazy Sunday morning, I decided to educate the kids on the lyrics of 'We didn't start the fire' by Billy Joel, as I had received a very interesting link in the mail which led to a video of the same song, showing each and every image that the lyrics of the song mentioned. The kids loved it.

Soon we got into it so much that we were singing at the top of our voices and dancing too. The bell rang just when we finished. (It didn't strike me then as to why it rang only when we finished but in retrospect it makes perfect sense!) It was the security guard. No—it's not what you think—he wasn't asking us to stop. He, in fact had enjoyed our performance so much (the curtains at the kitchen window were not drawn— an observation again made in retrospect) that he had decided not to interrupt it. Judging by the slightly amused and extremely entertained look on his face, the only thing missing was a placard in his hand which showed a perfect ten as a score, just like those judges show in the reality TV shows for singing and dancing. After he left, we practiced it 16 more times and then I got tired of it. The kids didn't, though. They were begging me to play it one more time.) I tried putting them on to Uptown girl and Piano man—but they got bored of that easily.

Then the three of us cooked *Biriyani* and made Mango milk shake. (The delicious, juicy, ripe, sweet Alphonso mangoes had started appearing in the market) After that the kids decided that they want to camp in the living room. (Why not—what is a Sunday without a little fun?) They pitched a tent there (not kidding—we have one of those child-friendly easy-to-open ones) and it was only 5 minutes of silence and muffled laughter later, that I realized they had pitched it next to the liquor cabinet and were busy playing their version of 'Bartender', my 6 year old daughter, putting her newly acquired reading abilities to good use, asking her brother whether he would have a Jack Daniels with a Blue Curacao! (Don't be shocked. Of course they did not open the cabinet—they were just pretending and reading the labels on the bottles.) I decided the fun for the day had gone too far and gently steered them towards their study books. Not steered actually, propelled, rocketed or pushed would be more like it. The bottom line is they did their studies. (Mission accomplished, mummy's guilt alleviated) They seem to lead a social life busier than mine and had to attend a birthday party. While they were away, the phone rang. It was my husband. (Thank God they were away—else I would not have been able to talk. Both would have fought to talk to papa.) He had called to say that he had reached his hotel, and wanted to know what I had been up to the whole day.

"Nothing much," I replied. You cannot describe the voyeuristic Security Guard, over an International call, can you?

I hate Sundays without him. (My husband I mean, not the Guard)

So that's what that Sunday went like. It wasn't one of the best weekends I had, but definitely it got filed in the mental cabinet where I file things worth remembering. Children will grow up and leave home. Arthritis or worse Alzheimers might prevent you from dancing like you used to.

That is why sometimes it is indeed great to dance like no one is watching, even if they are.

Divorce and other things

"Mommy what is the meaning of 'Divorce'?" asked my daughter who was six at that time.

It took me a minute to think what exactly I should say. Her brother who is 10, decided to answer her.

"Divorce means Mummy and Papa have to stay separately," he said.

"Well, it also means you are not married to that person anymore and you can marry again—you can choose whomever you want to marry," I added.

She thought for a minute and then exclaimed happily, "Cool! I didn't know that could be done."

The parenting instinct in me kicked in, alarmed at the prospect of my 6-year old forming an impression that 'Divorce is cool.' I decided to gently dispel the myth.

Just think, I told her, "You will have to choose between Mummy and Papa. We cannot stay together if we get divorced."

"Cool!" she exclaims again, "I will have two homes!"

"So, whom will you stay with?"

She takes one hard look at me, narrows her eyes and announces with an air of finality, "I will stay with Papa, of course."

I promptly made the saddest face that I could pull, doing my best imitation of the pained agony of Shah Rukh in Devdas. "Don't worry, Mommy," says her brother, "I will stay with you." My heart did a leap (at least one kid chose me), but a second too soon, because he almost immediately added, "But only if you buy me lots of toys." And I felt like P.T. Usha missing the Olympic medal by 1/400th of a second. Talk about exploitation! (This was like the tiny fine print that is hidden in what you thought was a fabulous deal.)

I pulled an even sadder face, and tried to look like Eeyeore in Winnie the Pooh, hoping to evoke some pity, some sympathy. I saw husband trying hard to not let the chuckle escape from his throat. "Okay," I said with dollops of melancholy wedged in with mustered angst, "Nobody loves me. So I shall run away."

"Mama, where to?" both children asked in unison. "Well—Egypt sounds good. Or maybe New Zealand. Maybe even Fiji—I have a friend there, you know."

"Cool! Can we go with you?"

"Oh no. Sorry. Both of you can't. I am running away with your Papa, you see. Both of you shall be packed off to your grand mom's place." (Sweet revenge!)

Both didn't know what to say to that. They looked at me in total dismay. They pleaded and begged and stated that they were only joking.

Now they're both convinced (with absolutely no room for even a teeny weenie doubt) that divorce isn't such a cool idea after all.

I am so pleased with myself. I am smiling and I am rubbing my hands in glee. And can anybody tell me why the Spiderman tune keeps playing in my head along with the words, "With great power comes great responsibility"?! Wait a minute! It should actually be, "With great responsibility comes a different kind of a power."

I think it is the power that comes when you decide to make your relationship work, *no matter what*. Once that power is attained, words like 'divorce' automatically get relegated to the trash bin which is ideally where they belong. After all, you had seen something in that person you fell in love with. Just because some things changed, it does not mean that one cannot work to make things go back to what they used to be. Too simplistic and idealistic a view? Perhaps. But nevertheless, it is worth thinking about.

Vegetable balls

A few years ago I was teaching at a pre school when this incident occurred. We had just had our Parent Teacher meetings. They can be exhausting. I had to patiently answer everything that the parents asked about their child. And parents, especially first timers can be very inquisitive, wanting to know each and every detail of what their precious angel does at school and whether he or she manages without the parent, and what delightful things he or she said. I too enjoy filling them in. I also have so much to share about the child and meeting with each parent takes at least 15 minutes.

Parents in the initial years are completely responsible for moulding their children. After all, they spend only three hours in a pre school and the rest of the time at home. The kind of inputs that a child receives at home makes such a difference. Some parents ruin their children's thinking skills and physical agility by only parking them in front of the television for long hours instead of having a healthy blend of outdoor and indoor activities. The kids really turn into zombies with no ability to imagine and think. Of course, I had to smile politely and tactfully convey the message across. I usually speak my mind—and so by the end of these meetings, I would be drained and washed out. It took such an effort to not say what I *really* thought!

So, when a friend and her husband offered to pick me up from school after the PTA meet and suggested we have lunch outside, was really glad. Her husband is a sweet guy and tells the funniest stories. He is a born leader. He is also naturally loud, forthright and the kind of person who will not hesitate to call a spade a spade. He talks very animatedly, using a lot of gestures to get his point across. He was also the Country head of his organization at that time. (He has moved to a much higher level now) In short, a kind of guy who leaves a lasting impression and the kind of guy you won't forget after meeting him.

We chose a nice Chinese restaurant—and decided to eat in the garden, as the weather was perfect. The children were at school and as much as we love our children, we also need adult company and we looked forward to catching up without a thousand interruptions.

My friend and I had been busy talking and we had told her husband to go ahead and order what he liked. He was hunched over the menu and was studying it intently so he could choose for the two ladies. The waiter came to take the order.

In his booming voice, with a hand gesture to match, my friend's husband asked, "Do you have Balls?"

There was a stunned silence all around and then every body burst out laughing. The waiter was trying hard to suppress his laughter. Even then he did not realize what he had said. He looked at both of us puzzled and asked, "What? Don't you like vegetable balls?"

That made us laugh even harder. We could barely speak.

To this day, when I go to a Chinese restaurant and read, "Vegetable balls in garlic sauce," I cannot help giggling.

And just for the record—I don't like vegetable balls. With or without garlic sauce!

Siblings without rivalry

Hermione Granger reminds me a lot of my daughter who is 6. She is a stickler for rules, almost always at the top of her class, bright, smart and like Hermione, if it is in a book, she can learn it! A teacher's dream student, to put it more simply. She rarely forgets to take anything that the teacher has said must be brought to class, even if the teacher herself has forgotten!

The school my children go to is a stickler for rules and is very strict about the dress code among a lot of other things. They had a winter uniform then —the tie and blazer being mandatory, apart from school belt and school ID card that each child had to compulsorily wear. (In addition the girls have a dark green hair band and dark green rubber bands for pony tails as well!) If any child is seen without any of the above mentioned things, they are labeled 'defaulters'.

But today, long after the children left for school, I discovered to my horror, that my daughter had forgotten to wear her blazer. The school does not allow parents inside the premises once the assembly bell rings. So there was no way I could reach it to her. I don't know how I did not notice, maybe it was because husband had to leave earlier than usual and I was pre-occupied. I felt bad when I discovered it, as it meant she would be punished as she had a special school assembly today. She hates being punished and being pulled up at school is the ultimate disaster, loss of face, end of the world, in her books. She cannot ever take it lightly.

There was nothing I could do except wait for them to come back from school. I was certain there would be huge tears rolling down her face when she came, and I would have to comfort her and hug her for at least forty five minutes, before she calmed down, the time required expertly calculated due to years of seasoned parenting!

I was wrong. They both came back from school, my daughter with a big smile on her face and wearing an over-sized blazer— her brother's! I was dumbstruck. After they boarded the bus to go to school, my son (he just turned 10) realized she would get punished and he took off his blazer and made her wear it. She was not caught— he was. He said he was a defaulter and owned up. I wondered what must have gone through his mind when he did that. I was so proud of him for protecting his younger sister. I was moved too, by his selfless act.

On some days , when they fight it looks as though they hate each other and would kill each other, if allowed to. Those are the days I wonder where I went wrong in raising them.

But today is one of those days, when I am going to bed with a happy-warm feeling, knowing that I must be doing something right!

Stay or Stray

A friend mailed me this beautiful story as an email forward, which was very moving. It can be found on many many sites on the Internet. I don't know who wrote it (and I tried hard to find out) but it is worth reading. It goes this way.

"When I got home that night as my wife served dinner, I held her hand and said, I've got something to tell you. She sat down and ate quietly. Again I observed the hurt in her eyes.

Suddenly I didn't know how to open my mouth. But I had to let her know what I was thinking. I want a divorce. I raised the topic calmly. She didn't seem to be annoyed by my words, instead she asked me softly, why? I avoided her question. This made her angry. She threw away the chopsticks and shouted at me, you are not a man!

That night, we didn't talk to each other. She was weeping. I knew

she wanted to find out what had happened to our marriage. But
could hardly give her a satisfactory answer; I had lost my heart t
a lovely girl called 'Someone'. I didn't love her anymore. I just pitie
her!

With a deep sense of guilt, I drafted a divorce agreement whic
stated that this was a divorce by mutual consent. She glanced at
and then tore it into pieces. The woman who had spent almost si
year of her life with me had become a stranger. I felt sorry for he
wasted time, resources and energy but I could not take back wha
I had said for I loved 'someone' else dearly.

Finally she cried loudly in front of me, which was what I had
expected to see. To me her cry was actually a kind of release. The
idea of divorce which had obsessed me for several weeks seemed
to be firmer and clearer now.

The next day, I came back home very late and found her writing
something at the table. I didn't have supper but went straight to
sleep and fell asleep very fast because I was tired after an eventful
day with 'someone'. When I woke up, she was still there at the
table, writing. I just did not care so I turned over and was asleep
again.

In the morning she presented her divorce conditions: she didn't
want anything from me, but needed a month's notice before the
divorce. She requested that in that one month we both struggle to
live as normal a life as possible. Her reasons were simple: our son
had his exams in a month's time and she didn't want to disturb him
with our broken marriage.

This was agreeable to me. But she had something more, she
asked me to recall how I had carried her into our bridal room on
our wedding day. She requested that everyday for the month's
duration I carry her out of our bedroom to the front door every

morning. I thought she was going crazy.

Just to make our last days together bearable I accepted her odd request.

I told 'someone' about my wife's divorce conditions. She laughed loudly and thought it was absurd. No matter what tricks she applies, she has to face the divorce, she said scornfully. My wife and I hadn't had any body contact since my divorce intention was explicitly expressed. So when I carried her out on the first day, we both appeared clumsy. Our son clapped behind us, daddy is holding mummy in his arms. His words brought me a sense of pain. From the bedroom to the sitting room, then to the door, I walked over ten meters with her in my arms. She closed her eyes and said softly; don't tell our son about the divorce. I nodded, feeling somewhat upset.

I put her down outside the door. She went to wait for the bus to work. I drove alone to the office.

On the second day, both of us acted much more easily. She leaned on my chest. I could smell the fragrance of her blouse. I realized that I hadn't looked at this woman carefully for a long time. I realized she was not young any more. There were fine wrinkles on her face, her hair was graying! Our marriage had taken its toll on her. For a minute I wondered what I had done to her.

On the fourth day, when I lifted her up, I felt a sense of intimacy returning. This was the woman who had given almost six years of her life to me. On the fifth and sixth day, I realized that our sense of intimacy was growing again. I didn't tell 'someone' this. It became easier to carry her as the month slipped by. Perhaps the everyday workout made me stronger.

She was choosing what to wear one morning. She tried on quite a few dresses but could not find a suitable one. Then she sighed, all my dresses have grown ' igger. I suddenly realized that she had grown so thin, that was the reason why I could carry her more easily. Suddenly it hit me; she had buried so much pain and bitterness in her heart.

Subconsciously I reached out and touched her head. Our son came in at the moment and said, Dad, it's time to carry mum out. To him, seeing his father carrying his mother out had become an essential part of his life. My wife gestured to our son to come closer and hugged him tightly. I turned my face away because I was afraid I might change my mind at this last minute. I then held her in my arms, walking from the bedroom, through the sitting room, to the hallway. Her hand rested on my neck softly and naturally. I held her body tightly; it was just like our wedding day.

But her much lighter weight made me sad. On the last day, when I held her in my arms, I could hardly move a step. Our son had gone to school. I held her tightly and said, I hadn't noticed that our life lacked intimacy. I drove to office... jumped out of the car swiftly without locking the door. I was afraid any delay would make me change my mind... I walked upstairs. 'Someone' opened the door and I said to her, sorry, 'someone', I do not want the divorce anymore.

She looked at me, astonished. Then she touched my forehead. 'Do you have a fever?' she said. I moved her hand off my head. 'Sorry, 'someone',' I said, 'I won't divorce. My married life was boring probably because she and I didn't value the details of our lives, not because we didn't love each other any more. Now I realize that since I carried her into my home on our wedding day I am supposed to hold her until death does us apart.'

'Someone' seemed to suddenly wake up. She gave me a loud slap and then slammed the door and burst into tears. I walked downstairs and drove away. At the floral shop on the way, I ordered a bouquet of flowers for my wife. The salesgirl asked me what to write on the card. I smiled and wrote:

"I'll carry you out every morning until death does us apart"

The small details of our lives are what really matter in a relationship. It is not the mansion, the car, the property, the bank balance that matters. These create an environment conducive for happiness but cannot give happiness in themselves. So find time to be your spouse's friend and do those little things for each other that build intimacy. Do have a real happy marriage!"

Growing apart and being completely disconnected from each other despite living together has happened to three people I know and they all have loving, smart and caring partners, on the face of it. It made me think as to why people, who are in committed relationships, stray. Those who have been married for long, (say 5 years or more) know that a certain level of comfort, intimacy and 'taking each other for granted', sets in.

To add to it, if you have young children, life together, gets even more complicated. Mornings are, almost always, a mad rush to get to work on time, to get the kids ready (and it is maddening how work will expand to fill up the available time—and how something will always crop up at the last minute, and how even when you have fool proofed everything , you can still be fooled!) Evenings are more rushed. Homework and dinner interspersed with that annoying thing called a blackberry, (which has you on a leash— always connected), rushed, to-the-point conversations and putting children to bed. Add to this, PTA meetings, grocery shopping, bills to be paid and more chores, chores, chores.

Not surprising then, that the 'fun element' in marriage dips drastically. Initial euphoria that young newlyweds (or couples in love) experience wears off slowly, without anyone even realizing it. (If you say it doesn't, I shall ask you how many years you have been married and whether you have kids!) Daily living takes its toll.

Enter a new person whom you meet at work or at the gym or even through a friend. This new person maybe very different from your spouse — physically and temperament or personality wise. This person might find you interesting and smart. (Which you are, but have forgotten in this daily business of 'life' and your partner hasn't told you that often enough.) This person may shower you with so much attention, time and make you feel so loved, wanted and happy. It is hard to resist such a temptation.

Many succumb. They are only human. It is their life, their choice and their call.

Besides they all have *their* reasons for making their life the way they want it to be.

Age Miracles

There seems to be a whole Industry thriving on making people want to look younger than they are. There are creams that promise to make your husband fall in love with you again. There are night creams and day creams. (How does the night cream know it is not supposed to work during the day, I wonder!) Images of wonderful looking people with impossibly thin youthful figures stare at us from the glossies. (There is a lot you can achieve with wrinkle-smoothening software, which has to be used on a photograph, not your face!) I think people who do look their age are lucky. They don't seem to face the kind of predicaments that I do.

"You don't look like a mother of two," is a line that I have heard as many times as you've heard *mauja hi mauja* playing full blast at parties, if you happen to live in India. It is mildly amusing at times. Most times it leaves me indignant and I am determined to prove my earned-after-really-hard-work-Motherhood status. After all, I opted for natural childbirth without any epidurals, breastfed both my babies for 18 months, gave up a full time job (couldn't bear to leave my precious babies in anybody else's care) and stayed up whole nights when they were unwell, read to them *Cat in a Hat* and *Jungle Book* at least a few hundred times, that if you woke me up in the middle of the night, I could start reciting them by rote, exactly, right down to the last word. The least I want is CREDIT that I AM indeed a mother—a devoted one at that! (See—I even named my blog 'Just a mother of two' to prove my mommy status.)

Worst is when I move to a new place. (And that happens every three years) I have to prove my status all over again. When we first moved to this city, the kids and I were taking a quick stroll around the complex which was to be our home. Mrs. Madan who must be in her sixties accosted us and said, "Welcome to the neighbourhood! You kids must be really excited." I smiled a warm smile, happy to have such friendly neighbours and nodded enthusiastically. She then looked at me and said, "So, which school do you all go to?"

I chose to ignore the 'you all' and said that they went to a school which was located nearby. "And what about you?" she asked. "Oh- I just stay at home and look after them. I am their mom."

"You are kidding me."

"I am not."

I don't think she believed me—she just smiled, shook her head and walked away.

Another time, the door bell rang and the guy who delivers the courier asked me to get my mom's signature (and it was a letter addressed to me). I glared at him and roared, "I am THE MOM here." Poor guy must have got a fright. Out of the corner of my eye I could see my husband doubling up with laughter on the sofa. I was not amused.

A few years back, a group of us decided to have a woman's night out. Most of us had two kids and our husbands had agreed to baby sit. Excitedly, feeling like college kids we crept out, all dolled up in 'hip clothes' giggling, laughing. I was feeling great till the guy at the pub stopped me and said, "Under 18 not allowed." I had to show my drivers license to prove my age. (The moron—I have been driving a car for 18 years now.) And my friends couldn't stop laughing. They assured him that I was indeed a mom and well over 18. "She just looks like a kid," they elaborated. (I call it rubbing salt to the wound and they claim they were helping me.)

When I was visiting my mom in Kerala, (Most moms in Kerala wear sarees –and I wear them only on special occasions) we bumped into a lady from the neighbourhood. She sweetly asked, "*Mol ethu classila paddikyune?*" (Roughly translated, "Baby, which grade are you studying in?")

With a face as straight as I could muster, I answered, "*Molde Paddithamokke kazhinju. Kalyanam ayi. Randu kuttikalu undu.*" (Baby has finished studies, is married and has two kids.)

Her eyes popped, jaw dropped open. Then she burst into laughter and apologized—and that soothed my somewhat indignant ego.

When I have to go to the shops nearby, I prefer to use my two-wheeler. At traffic junctions, it is horrifying to see the college guys checking me out—and one audacious fool had the guts to wink at me. "A** hole," I said "I have a son who will be as old as you in a few years." And I looked right back at him, meeting him in the eye—daring him. The light changed and he sped away.

So, if you look your age when you reach your forties or look much older even though you are only in your thirties, don't even think of Botox or those magic creams that promise you 'Age miracles.' Let me assure you—they just aren't worth it! (Unless they promise to make you look older, that is.)

And in any case, I constantly remind myself that external beauty like youth is only fleeting. One cannot be young forever. Age is going to catch up with every single one of us. (Unless you die, in which case, it won't matter.) As each second ticks by, we are that much older. So what would really make a difference is to have a big smile on your face, truly rejoice when good things happen and to spend time with the ones you love, savoring and cherishing even small moments.

The Gift of a Sibling

They say blood is thicker than water. I think they are right. If you hail from a time when it was the norm to have two or three children, then you would probably agree whole heartedly about the importance of growing up with siblings. These days however, families seem to have shrunk and many parents opt for a single child.

My brother and I share a close bond like many siblings do. Research has proved that the sibling relationship has a power to influence who we are and what we turn into as adults. Many of my friends admit to a big influence that their older sibling had in influencing their choice of career.

I fail to understand how even such a deep bond becomes diluted when tainted with money. There are many cases of fights over property, businesses and other material things. How do siblings turn into enemies? Why does greed consume everything?

Why don't we remember that no matter how much money you have or you don't have, you still need four pall bearers to carry you on your last journey and *one of them would most probably be your sibling?*

There are countless childhood memories that I cherish which I share with my brother. But the one that we still talk about whenever we meet is this one.

It was a long time ago, when kids still collected postage stamps and sea shells from the beach. What I owned was a prized possession— a triangular shaped postage stamp, with a beautiful picture of a rocket on it. The country was Mongolia. It raised my status among my peers, the other kids, the stamp collectors.

"She has a triangular stamp."

"From Mongolia!"

"Can we, please, have a look at it?"

There were hushed and awed whispers, from the other kids, whenever I took out the stamp album. I felt like a queen. Nobody else had a triangular postage stamp. Nor a stamp with a picture of a rocket on it, for that matter. It was rare, those days.

My little brother used to longingly look at it. I wouldn't even let him touch my coveted stamp album. It was safely locked and the key deposited with mom, if I wasn't around.

My brother was not one to give up so easily. What he wanted, he usually got. He waited for a chance. Patiently.

It came when we were returning from school, one day. I was with a friend, walking ahead and he was trailing behind us, as usual.

The green raw mangoes, hanging in Mr. Sharma's garden, just above his gate, were irresistible. Anyone who has eaten sour green mangoes will know just how much they tempt.

My friend suggested that we pluck a few. She and I climbed the gate and reached out, and started plucking the green mangoes. What we did not anticipate was Mrs. Sharma's hawk-like watch over her precious mangoes.

"Hey, you thieves!" she roared. And then a second later, "I know you—you are Mr. Kamath's daughter, aren't you?"

I did not answer. We ran (with the mangoes). We did not slow down, till we reached the bus stop.

Then we burst into laughter.

My brother had been a silent observer.

"Here!" I held out a green mango.

He looked at it for a second. His mouth watered at the sight. But he shook his head.

"No," he said. Then, he uttered the dreaded words, "I will tell Mom what you did today"

"Please, please, please, don't," I begged, pleaded.

We knew what was in store, had our mom found out that I had *stolen* Mangoes. That, too, from someone whom they knew.

When we reached home, I asked my mother for the key, to take out my stamp album. She was surprised when she saw me giving my coveted Mongolia rocket stamp to my brother.

"But why?" my mother had asked in surprise.

"Just like that, Ma. I felt like giving him a gift."

Later, that day, the phone rang.

It was Mrs. Sharma, asking to speak to my mother.

Phone therapy

Many scientists have spent valuable time, resources and energy to prove something that we knew all along. Women really do talk more than men. The average woman coughs up 20,000 words in a day compared to a miserable 7000 by men. That is almost 13000 words more! Studies also suggest that women speak more quickly, devote more brain power to talking and actually get a high out of hearing their own voices. And, if that wasn't enough, they go on to say that simple act of talking triggers a flood of brain chemicals which give women a rush similar to that felt by heroin addicts when they get a high! I do not know how much of it to believe, despite being medically proven and all that. But heart of hearts I have a niggling feeling that they are right.

It was in the middle of that Thank-God-Husband-and kids-have-left-and-I-can-read-the-newspaper-in-peace cup of coffee that my best friend called.

What she said, or what I thought she said made me gulp the scalding liquid in a single swig.

"Uh—Whaaaaat?" I managed after a stunned 3 second silence.

"I said I was addicted to phone," she said.

"Ooooh!" The relief was obvious in my tone. I had thought she said porn!

Being thirty-something, plummeting headlong without any brakes into forties at rapid, breakneck speed like a player on GTA running from the cop he just killed, makes you do strange things at times, and I had initially attributed what I thought was her shocking revelation into that category. Knowing that it was only the harmless, innocuous telephone she was addicted to, somewhat calmed my caffeine-charged jangled nerves. I could understand as I was guilty of the same.

Thank God for the telephone. No, make that Thank you Alexander Graham Bell, Airtel, Vodafone, Tata Indicom, BSNL, Ministry of Telecommunications or whoever it is that provides you the connectivity.

How would we have survived without it? How could our almost-as-close-as-sisters, inseparable, crazy-as-lunatic, mad, filled-with-laughter friendship have survived without it?

When she was living in Spain, she used to call me and we would talk for two hours and ten minutes (sometimes two hours and forty five) at a stretch. We discovered the law of International telephony. The geographical distance and the forbiddingly high calling rates are directly proportional to the urgency and the need to talk to your best friend. There were so many things that we just HAD to discuss. It couldn't wait. Since I didn't have International Dialing, I would often go to the public telephone booth and call her. Half the time, I had to listen impatiently to some gibberish in Spanish at the end of which there would be a beep and invariably my message to the answering machine would be, "Nothing important. Just wanted to talk."

Of course, we both knew that it translated to: "Where the hell are you? Give me a call right now."

Sometimes this is how the conversations would go.

She: "Hey, Are you busy?"

Me: "No—not really." (I would have managed to switch off the stove, calm a crying baby, and saved a word document I was working on, and yelled out to whoever was ringing the doorbell that I would open in 5 minutes, just so I could answer her call)

She: "I just called—Nothing important." (I would know that it was really important and she had to tell me or she would burst) Then she would spill out whatever was bothering her, or sometimes it would be the other way round. I would speak and she would listen.

We both moved cities and we now live only 180 kilometers from each other. We have discovered another law of telephony. Closer you live to each other, and cheaper the call rates, the more number of times you call. Needless to say, the once-a-day telephone call is mandatory when the day starts. And throughout the day, the regular short updates on anything perceived important. I think we still average two-and-a-half hours!

Our poor husbands pretend to blissfully not mind. (What choice do they have anyways?) We have convinced them, or we think we have convinced them that talking to each other is as essential and important as watching a cricket match between India and Pakistan or the IPL matches. Not to say, we have also thrown in the fringe benefit of not having to pay shrink bills as talking to best friend therapy is as effective as seeing a shrink.

What amazes me is despite all this talking, we still have so much to say. It seems to be almost endless. When we go over to stay at each other's homes, we can still talk through the night. In the background, we are vaguely aware of our spouses pretending not to listen, but ears perked, hanging intensely to every word, lest they miss something.

I cannot talk like this to anyone else. At least, not this much! It is rarely that you can connect at every level to someone. It is even rarer, as you grow older, to have the freedom to pick up the phone and call them for the sixth time in a day, knowing they will welcome the call as eagerly. I thought that kind of stuff and the concept of 'best friend' ended with teenage and did not manifest in mature, calm, composed, thirty-something-hurling-into-forties seasoned mothers of two. I am so glad, thankful and happy that I was wrong!

And maybe I now grudgingly admit, *just maybe,* the scientists were right after all.

Little details

On Saturday, I was compelled to attend a children's birthday party. Compelled, because the hostess very clearly told me that it wasn't just a children's party and the parents are invited as well. 'Parent' in my case, as husband was overseas, on an assignment. This naturally left me to do the needful—in this case to attend the party and to pretend I am enjoying.

Don't get me wrong. I'm not anti-social and I *try* not to be a snob. But a children's birthday party, with 40 screaming, out-of-control kids playing 'pass the parcel' and 'musical chairs' is definitely not my idea of fun. I work with kids and really enjoy the company of children. But at most parties, they turn into little uncontrollable monsters.

My children, of course were excited and since their dad was out of town, the prospect of spending a Saturday evening, without my own two (oh yes—they had decided that they would go to the party whether or not I accompanied them—they have a mind of their own, began to look less and less appealing as the evening progressed and I ended up attending the party—the party for kids *and* parents.

The kids were having a whale of a time, and were really enjoying themselves. I was beginning to feel happy that I was attending it, (though I suspect that had largely to do with the Vodka that I was having) when I was buttonholed by a guest who introduced himself as Rakesh or Rajesh or Ramesh or something like that.(It did not make a difference to me as he was neither good looking nor intelligent and not even a good conversationalist. In short, he did not interest me at all) He wedged his chair next to mine, in such a way, that I had no choice but to make polite talk—or rather respond to his Spanish inquisition. I desperately hoped that one of the children would rescue me with a "Mummy! Can you please come here, **RIGHT NOW**?" A plea which I usually hear 50 times a day, but no such luck today. They were too busy having fun.

My son (who was 9 at that time) did come up to me, but only to shove a packet in my hand which contained some goodies which he had won. And before I could say anything, he had run off, whereupon the buttonholer asked me inquisitively, "Your brother?"

Either he was very drunk or very foolish, or very shortsighted or very so wanted to flatter me.

I answered dead pan, "No, my son."

"You are kidding!"

"No, I am not. Unless the whole nine months that I carried him was an impossibly conjured up vision by Houdini or unless I am delusional."

That took a moment to sink in and he laughed uncontrollably. I felt like an animal trapped in quicksand, wanting to get out, but getting buried deeper.

He asked me my name (never mind that when he introduced himself, I had not volunteered any details about me—but a little detail like that did not bother him) and then said, "Ooh—pretty!" (I have been hearing that line for the past 20 years. Very unoriginal. Very boring. Very irritating.) He proceeded to tell me that he lived in the US of A, and was visiting India. He prattled on about how good the infrastructure in the US is (I am sure it is) and how miserable India is, in comparison.

One thing that nettles me is someone talking ill of my country. (And in this case his own country too.) He told me he lived in Texas, Plano and proceeded to tell me what a marvelous place it is, and how he had the choice of five places, while moving to the US and why he chose Texas. I couldn't even feign polite interest. But little details like that did not bother him. When he launched into a diatribe about how the 'Indian Government does nothing' I just couldn't keep quiet anymore.

What I felt like doing was emptying the Vodka I was having on his head. But that would have been a waste of good Vodka—and I was sure a little detail like that would not bother him! So I did the next best thing. Quoted statistics. I told him that the Government of India had established IDFC (Infrastructure Development Finance Corporation) and also that India currently has 8 international and more than 88 domestic airports. And that India's road networking covers 2.9 million kilometers, the third largest in the world, and also that Indian Railways is the second largest system in the world under a single management, with an extensive network of 62,725 kilometers. (Phew!) [Who did he think made all these?]

The data I had memorized for my last exam, surprisingly, came to my rescue, probably spurred by the Vodka I was having and the fervour of patriotism I was feeling.

But— you guessed it—little details like this did not seem to affect him. It did buy me a few fractions of nano seconds, though. My desperation to escape made me stand up and wave enthusiastically to a non-existent person across the room.

And I made my getaway, feeling triumphant, with my head held high, having defended the honour of my country.

It is definitely good to remember and recall details. But it is even better to pretend to be schizophrenic.

A gift for you!

Have you ever wondered what to gift your girlfriend? Or have you wondered what to give that 'I-think-it is-a crush-but-I am-not-so-sure' kind of a friend? If you have, welcome to the club. You are not alone.

Throughout the animal kingdom, the males of the species have always wooed the females. Mating rituals in the animal kingdom are very fascinating as they are natural. A single male grasshopper has more than 400 songs in his repertoire—I think enough to give Elvis Presley *and* Himesh Reshmaiyya put together a complex of being woefully inadequate! Researchers have proved that Blue whales produce low frequency repetitive booming calls to attract females and ward off other males.

When we happened to visit a wildlife sanctuary we were able to watch the mating ritual of the Red deer. We saw two stags fighting with each other, while the female in question stood watching, seemingly disinterested.

When I first discovered this I could not help observing how similar humans are, despite all the advancement, technological progress and sophistication. Countless movies have revolved around the theme of two males competing for a single female.

What amused me no end was the rituals that praying mantises follow. They are known for a strange mating ritual. The females are said to behead and devour their partners, before, during or after mating. In fact, more often than not, males avoid being eaten through a combination of caution and speed.

To win acceptance, some male insects (like the scorpion fly) present the potential mates with nuptial gifts, during courtship. Generally, the gifts take the form of food, but may also be merely empty packages, designed to stimulate the female's interest or divert her attention during mating.

Before searching for a mate, many male flies kill prey, and then enclose the remains in cases made from silk or a frothy secretion. Carrying the light weight cases to a mating site, the males pass them to the females, who clasp the gifts to their abdomens. While she is occupied, the female all but ignores the male, as he proceeds to couple with her.

Among the more advanced species of insects, males present only empty cases or bits of petals or leaves, which serve the same purpose. Empty—can you imagine! How clever is that! (How can the females get fooled so easily?)

It made me smile to think that ladies, when they open their valentine gifts have to be really, *really* careful. And it doesn't hurt the guys to be prepared to run for their lives!

After all, the human species seems to have traits of all of the above (even the killing bit in some extreme cases).

What happened to my friend Maya was not exactly like the above, but it did involve gifts. We were in college and I was visiting her at her hostel at that time. Staying in a hostel gives you all kind of opportunities to be away from the prying eyes of parents and, passing off a boy friend as a cousin or a family member is as easy as downing a tequila shot. It is intimidating only the first time. After that, the high you get hooks you.

Her guy had gifted her forty cute little teddy bears. Forty! She just couldn't believe it. He had never given her any gift before and this was so overwhelming. He had brought them all in a box and left it for her that morning. He had to go to office (he was working, while we were in our final year) and had left a note saying he would visit in the evening.

Maya was delighted. Soft toys always melt women, no matter what their age—and forty of them in a box, is so overwhelming. All of us gathered around her admiring the cute little fellas. Some of us asked her for one, and Maya being the generous soul that she is, began distributing them to whoever was in her good books at that point of time and whoever pleaded hard enough. Soon she was left with about eleven and she was content with that. After all, what will you do with forty identical bears who vary a little only in colour?

Her boy friend came in the evening as promised. Maya was beaming. He reveled in the warmth.

"So, did you like them? And did your friends like them?" he asked.

"How did you know that I'd give them to my friends?" she retorted.

"Oh, I know you women ' he replied with a wave of the hand.

She smiled contentedly. The enjoyed the silence that only two people comfortable with each othe can.

Then he said, "So, where is the money?"

"What money?" she asked

"The money for the bears," he said, " I had left them with you for selling them to your friends. I knew your friends would like them. A friend of mine has started a new gift store," he said.

Both of us did not know what to say to that. We looked hard to see if he was joking.

He wasn't.

You can imagine what must have happened after that!

****

Gift suggestions for a woman, if you are a man: You can classify them into three categories, depending on what kind of a woman she is.

Romantic gift, Just- a-good-friend gift and Experience gift.

Romantic gifts could include jewellery, luxury chocolates, sexy lingerie, symbols of love and diamonds.

Just-a-good-friend gifts could be books, a funky t-shirt, something for the home, a watch, pens, something for the office desk, funny fridge magnets, posters, paintings.

Experience gifts could be signing her up for an Art class/Guitar class, booking a vacation in a small, quaint undiscovered place, signing up for paragliding (if she is the adventurous sort) or scuba diving and signing up for a hiking tour.

Gift suggestions for a Man, if you are a woman: Turn up naked!

When life tricks you

There's a grumpy old man who lives in the neighbourhood. I have never seen him smile. I don't think anyone has. He saunters around the whole residential complex like a displeased dictator surveying his province. He looks angry, irritated and ready to bite off your head, if you dare so much as meet his eye. I have never seen anyone greeting him or talking to him.

I tried to, at first, when I moved in to this neighbourhood. I am like that. I like to greet neighbours. I like to spread cheer. I like to at least say a hello to the people I meet. My enthusiastic 'Good mornings' or 'Good evenings' were met with a curt nod of the head—as though he was asking me how I dared break the invisible wall of 'Leave me alone' that he had created for himself. I persisted for about a month or so—then I gave up. I still greet him though, if eye contact is unavoidable when I pass him. But most of the time I turn the other way. I don't need grouches or drains spoiling my day.

The old man lives with his wife, son, daughter-in-law and their two children. They invited us for a cup of tea the other day. I dreaded accepting the invitation as I knew the old man would be there. I did not want to meet him or talk to him. To my pleasant surprise he wasn't around.

The old man's wife got talking to me. She is very jovial and completely opposite of her husband. She is helpful, kind and courteous. She also talks a lot. Perhaps she is lonely or perhaps she finds me a good listener. (I always listen—it means I don't have to answer too many questions about myself!) She told me about their life before they moved to this place. She told me a lot of things. She told me they had lost an adult son who had been mentally challenged. They had spent years caring for him, taking him to a special school, bringing him back, looking after him. She knew a lot about caring for people with special needs.

Sometimes when my two normal, healthy children fight and do not listen to me and drive me up the wall, I feel angry, like all parents, and lose my cool. I wondered how this couple coped with caring for a fully grown adult who could not do anything for himself and also another child with normal needs. I felt her pain as she spoke about the long years that had gone into caring for her adult son. To get away from the memories, they had sold that house and moved here, after he had died.

For the first time, I began realizing what a big burden the old man must have carried in his younger years. No wonder he was this way. Perhaps the years took their toll on him. But the very next instant I couldn't help thinking that his wife too had gone through the same thing. As a mother, perhaps her pain was greater. Yet her attitude to life was so completely different from his.

It made me think about an email forward that I received. It was written by Mary Sullivan. (I tried hard to track down the right Mary Sullivan who wrote it so I could take permission to reproduce it here, but failed. I did manage to contact another Mary Sullivan though.) Anyway, that is digressing from the topic. This is what it said:

"A young woman went to her mother and told her about her life and how things were so hard for her. She did not know how she was going to make it and wanted to give up, She was tired of fighting and struggling. It seemed as one problem was solved, a new one arose. Her mother took her to the kitchen. She filled three pots with water and placed each on a high fire. Soon the pots came to boil. In the first she placed carrots, in the second she placed eggs, and in the last she placed ground coffee beans. She let them sit and boil, without saying a word. In about twenty minutes she turned off the burners. She fished the carrots out and placed them in a bowl. She pulled the eggs out and placed them in a bowl. Then she ladled the coffee out and placed it in a bowl. Turning to her daughter, she asked, 'Tell me what you see.'

'Carrots, eggs, and coffee,' she replied.

Her mother brought her closer and asked her to feel the carrots. She did and noted that they were soft. The mother then asked the daughter to take an egg and break it. After pulling off the shell, she observed the hard boiled egg.

Finally, the mother asked the daughter to sip the coffee. The daughter smiled as she tasted its rich aroma. The daughter then asked, 'What does it mean, mother?'

Her mother explained that each of these objects had faced the same adversity: boiling water. Each reacted differently. The carrot went in strong, hard, and unrelenting. However, after being subjected to the boiling water, it softened and became weak The egg had been fragile. Its thin outer shell had protected its liquid interior, but after sitting through the boiling water, its inside became hardened. The ground coffee beans were unique, however. After they were in the boiling water, they had changed the water.

'Which are you?' she asked her daughter. 'When adversity knocks on your door, how do you respond? Are you a carrot, an egg or a coffee bean?'

Think of this: Which am I? Am I the carrot that seems strong, but with pain and adversity do I wilt and become soft and lose my strength?

Am I the egg that starts with a malleable heart, but changes with the heat? Did I have a fluid spirit, but after a death, a breakup, a financial hardship or some other trial, have I become hardened and stiff? Does my shell look the same, but on the inside am I bitter and tough with a stiff spirit and hardened heart?

Or am I like the coffee bean? The bean actually changes the hot water, the very circumstance that brings the pain. When the water gets hot, it releases the fragrance and flavor. If you are like the bean, when things are at their worst, you get better and change the situation around you. When the hour is the darkest and trials are their greatest do you elevate yourself to another level?

How do you handle adversity? Are you a carrot, an egg or a coffee bean?

May you have enough happiness to make you sweet, enough trials to make you strong, enough sorrow to keep you human and enough hope to make you happy.

The happiest of people don't necessarily have the best of everything; they just make the most of everything that comes along their way. The brightest future will always be based on a forgotten past; you can't go forward in life until you let go of your past failures and heartaches.

When you were born, you were crying and everyone around you was smiling.

Live your life so that at the end, you're the one who is smiling and everyone around you is crying."

That day when I came home, I thought about the old man and his wife for a long time. She was indeed a coffee bean. I looked at the old man, too, differently—he couldn't help being what he was—and I made a mental note to resume greeting him everyday.

Double Whammy

In those days, about thirteen years back, Internet had not penetrated India as much as it has now. Computer courses were hailed as the courses of the future. The technological revolution hadn't yet taken place. I was working at a computer education centre, looking after placements. We used to still rely on printed reports and I had to submit one the next day, at the monthly meeting of all the centers. I had a meeting scheduled for the next day. I was in a tearing hurry to take a print out. To prevent unauthorized use (as there were a lot of students) the dot matrix printer that the centre had was located right next to the General Manager's desk. That particular day, there were some exams going on and I could not find any machine free to work on. Laptops were a big luxury back then, unlike today. I didn't know what to do. Finally one of the faculty members told me he could let me use his machine for about 15 minutes, and I jumped at the chance as eagerly as those singers grab the mike in the auditions for 'Indian idol'. Since it did not have a printer connected to it, I put the contents into a floppy (Pen drives were also a big luxury back then and I don't think I had even heard of one) and took it to the machine that was connected to the printer, which was again occupied by another faculty member. I waited and waited, and finally he said he was going out for a smoke and yes, I could use it to take a print out. He logged out. I put the floppy in. It wasn't going in easily. It was an old machine— So I pushed it a little harder and it obliged. I clicked on the icon which showed the floppy drive. At that moment, the screen flickered and it went blank. I didn't know what to do. I tried retrieving my data. No use. I was in a hurry too as a delay here would mean my missing the usual train that I caught to reach home.

The General Manager Mr. Shah was a towering personality, tall, dark, hefty with a huge moustache to boot. On normal days he intimidated people. On a day like this I don't know how he would have reacted. His reactions are usually unpredictable, a bit like the London weather. But the Gods of moods do have a sense of humour and that day he actually offered to help me. (May be because he saw my expression—I was almost ready to burst into tears and very desperate to get that print out). I looked at my watch and realized that I had already missed my train home. He came and tried retrieving it. No use.

Then the guy who had gone for a smoke came back. He was supposed to be an expert. He too tired and was puzzled.

Then he said we could try taking out the floppy and putting it back in—it might work. So he pressed the eject button. The floppy seemed to be stuck. He tried taking it out—but it was jammed. I was ready to pull out my hair. But the General Manager was determined that I should get my print out. So he summoned the Hardware Engineer. The faculty member who had allowed me to use the machine was giving me a glare and I looked at him helplessly, a bit apologetic that his work was now getting held up because of me.

The Hardware Engineer came—and he opened up the machine. He discovered what the problem was. He said, "How in the world did you manage this?"

It was one of the most embarrassing moments of my life. I wished the Earth could open up and swallow me.

In addition to the floppy already existing in the machine I had also managed to push in mine! There were TWO floppies in the same drive!

I could see the faculty member shaking his head, suppressing a smile and the General Manager doing the same thing.

To this day I don't know how I could have done such a stupid thing.

I still hate floppies and have never used them.

I am sure everybody else has forgotten about that incident now. (Well, unless they happen to read my book!) At that time, it seemed like a big deal to me. It seemed like I would not be able to show my face in the office the next day.

Surprisingly the only person who was most affected was me and today I have realized that most people are too busy leading their own lives to bother about laughing at you.

What seems very important and larger than life to you may not even make a small difference for others. I did not know it then, but

I know now that the best thing to do when such things happen is simply to join in the laughter and then treat it like yesterday's newspaper.

Truth is stranger than fiction

Sometimes life can be full of bizarre coincidences that have no explanation. Truth can really be stranger than fiction. In this incident that I am going to narrate to you, it can be verified as there is documented evidence to prove the strange coincidence.

The traditional Indian Calendar that has been in use for centuries uses phases of moon, position of planets and also mentions the major festivals, their significance and a lot more. 'Pournami' is the full moon day and it is considered significant. It is not very common for Pournami to occur on the same date as the English or Gregorian Calendar the following month. For example, if Pournami is on the 15th of this month, the next month it may be on 16th or 14th or even 13th or 17th (owing to the fact that each month in Gregorian calendar has different number of days—sometimes 31, sometimes 30, or 28 in case of February (and 29 if it is a leap year)

Anyway, to cut a long story short, it was on a Pournami that my dad died. The date was 7th of September 2006. He passed away at 8.30 pm. His plane tickets were booked to come to Mumbai as my brother's wife was expecting their first baby at that time and was due to deliver in the first week of October. He never made the journey. He was so looking forward to it, and we used to speak on the phone almost everyday and he would tell me how eager he was to visit us all.

My brother and I spent about 20 days with my mom, after performing the last rites. We came back in the last week of September and I returned home.

We were now counting the days till my brother's wife delivered. I wondered how much more emotional stress my brother could take. Here on one side, he had just performed the last rites of his dad— and on the other, he was going to become a first time father himself. Imagine the emotional turmoil he would have been going through. What really saddened me was that my dad would never get to see his baby.

On 7th of October, early in the morning, my brother called to say that his wife was getting labour pains and was in the hospital. He asked me if I realized that it was exactly one month since dad died. (I hadn't.) To this day, I don't know what made me say it, but when he said that, I replied that his baby would come out at 8:30 p.m. (as that was the time that my dad had died.) The whole day we were waiting anxiously for the delivery to happen. Imagine my astonishment, when my brother called again at around 8:45 pm to say that his wife had delivered a baby girl, and the time of birth was 8:30 pm! *And it was a normal delivery.*

I looked at the Indian calendar and discovered another spine chilling fact. It was a full moon night—a Pournami!

What an eerie coincidence that time of birth matched time of death, both were full moon nights, both 7th of the month—and the Pournami too coincided with the Gregorian date that month. Truth is sometimes truly stranger than fiction—and if it hadn't happened to me, I'd have probably not even believed it.

The attachment I feel to this child is overwhelming and irrationally deep. I simply adore this baby. She delights me, brings me so much happiness and she continues to be one of the candies in my life.

I really do not know whether to believe in life after death or reincarnation. But coincidences like these, give one the strength to hope and to go on.

The stranger

He is a complete stranger. I do not even know his name. Yet his face, and more importantly his act of kindness, has occupied space in my memory. Let me tell you why.

Eruveli is a small village deep inside Kerala—and like all small villages there, it is lush green, verdant, peaceful and so unhurried. It is nature at its best. My children and I love visiting this place. We were taking a walk through the paddy fields, one day. Suddenly, my children spied two kids (baby goats) frolicking across the field. If you have observed them, you know how cute they look—and how they jump sideways and how fast they are.

We stood staring, amused at their antics. My daughter exclaimed, "Mama—so cute—I wish I could hold them."

I told her it would be impossible to catch them, but they were welcome to try. My children tried going near them, but they bounded away in no time. The paddy field was huge, probably three times the size of a football pitch, and there was no way my kids could outrun the goat kids.

Suddenly this man emerged. He had been watching us, the 'city dwellers', with amusement. He was bare-chested, dressed in traditional clothes (a *lungi*). He was pleased that I could speak his language. He said the goat kids belonged to him and his children too loved to pet them. That was the reason he had bought them. He asked if my children would like to hold them. I told him they would be delighted, as these are things we do not get to do in the city.

He then chased the goat kids around the paddy field. It wasn't an easy task and in an expert manner, managed to catch them. He then gave one to my son and one to my daughter. To say my children were overjoyed is to put it mildly!

I wanted to click his picture and he obliged. I was moved by the effort he made, just to make my children happy.

We left the paddy field, with a happy warm feeling—and memories to last a lifetime. All because, a complete stranger chose to do a random act of kindness, just to make two children happy.

Smile — Tomorrow may be worse!

Kids really say the darndest things. And not just on a Bill Cosby show. It is amazing, at times, how much insight they have. And how piercingly true their words are. If you have your own children, you probably have similar tales to narrate.

If you don't here is what I am talking about.

I was feeling a bit down, as I was thinking about my husband leaving for an overseas assignment early next morning.

The prospect of being alone with the kids, without him, was making me feel so low that I wanted an extension ladder to get out of it. It came in the form of my 6 year old daughter.

"Mommy! Are you upset because your dad died and you are missing him?" (The usual reason whenever they see me on the verge of tears)

"No, baby. Today I am upset because your papa is leaving early tomorrow morning and I'm going to miss him really bad."

She perked up instantly and said in a bright voice, "Oh! Is that all? He is not yet dead. He will come back soon! Smile, Mommy. You look better when you smile."

I did not smile.

I burst out laughing.

What women want

A guide for men to keep that special woman in their life permanently happy and hooked!

Most men are clueless as to what women want. They say women confuse them. They say women are hard to understand. They say women are perplexing creatures. It would be nice if someone told them exactly what women want (as many are not endowed with powers that Mel Gibson had in the movie 'What women want'). Reams and reams have been dedicated to this topic. It has been the subject of endless discussions. Many of my male friends told me that if only women told them what they want, relationships between them could improve a great deal. So I wrote this somewhat tongue-in-cheek letter, which many of my female friends forwarded to the men in their lives.

Dear boyfriend/husband/current man in my life,

When we see you at the end of the day, and say, "I have had a rea[l]
hard day today," just hold us and give us a hug instead of askin[g]
"Oh, really, what happened?"

Sometimes, we don't want you to make things right, we just ne[ed]
a hug.

When we ask you if that gorgeous, slimmer lady is more attracti[ve]
than us, please say "Yes, but I'm sure she isn't as great a wife/moth[er]
as you are."

Sometimes, we just want to be assured that we still matter.

When we ask you if we look fat in an outfit, please say, "It sui[ts]
you well." If it really looks horrible, please say, "I think you will loo[k]
better in that other outfit."

Sometimes, we just need a little straight talk.

When we ask you if you mind taking us out, even though there i[s]
a cricket match on TV, please be honest and fix a time when it wil[l]
not interfere with your match watching. Taking us out and the[n]
glancing at your watch every five minutes, makes us feel guilty[.]
Sometimes, we appreciate honesty too!

When we ask you if you miss us, when you go on those outstation
trips, please lie a bit and say that you cannot wait to get back home,
even if you are having a great time, at a five star hotel paid for by the
company.

Sometimes, we need to hear a bit of a lie too!

When we tell you that another guy seems nice, we aren't thinking of getting into bed with him. We are probably thinking that he would make a nice husband for that still single girl-friend of ours. We are not mentally comparing you.

Sometimes, at least sometimes, don't doubt our intentions!

When you are driving us back home after a nice dinner at a restaurant and we ask you, "Do you want to stop for coffee?" please say yes, even if you really do not want coffee, because it means we are asking as we want to stop!

Sometimes, we like you to mind-read too!

When we sometimes complain to you about our problems, please do NOT give us solutions.

Sometimes, we just want you to listen and be sympathetic.

See—it is so easy to please us—how can you say you don't understand women.

With love,

The woman in your life

To this letter, this is what my husband replied.

What men want

(The principles of being what we are - Happy and hooked (to every woman)

Dear Girlfriend/Wife/Better half / Current Women in my life/ Neighbour/ And the many more that will come into my Life,

At the end of the day when we come back from office, we too are tired. We have dealt with a number of species of animals which should ideally have been made extinct (read nasty bosses, suppliers, customers!), different from the nice type of people that we are. A hug from you is what we want.

We are all like Mahatma Gandhi and believe in Equality (especially amongst women). When we say that a woman is gorgeous we are referring to her inner beauty. Not in all cases do we like size zero — in most cases there has to be some matter. Moreover you do matter, but her matter is also worth considering.

We always talk straight. If you think you look fat in the dress, then the other dress too may not be appropriate. And, it is not the fault of the dress, by the way. If you don't like an honest answer then why on earth do you raise the question?

The whole of this year and the next have cricket matches already scheduled, including the IPL all year round. We will therefore definitely schedule some time to go out in 2010 assuming the BCCI and ICC go to sleep and do not fix up any further tournaments. And speaking of guilt, how is it that you never feel guilty while you are constantly jabbering on the phone with your girlfriends (and maybe boyfriends) on those short / long distance calls, and ignore our presence?

When we go traveling we use the 5 Star Hotels only for sleeping. The hectic day's work dealing with animals leaves us no time to come back and dream of you and the house. And yes, we do yearn to come back home as soon as possible, but we need to work that extra bit harder to pay those telephone and add-on credit card bills..

The issue is not whether we think you are thinking of getting into bed with the other guy. The issue is that he is thinking. So please refrain from coming up with such oxymorons while discussing things with us - "the other guy being a good husband". Good husbands, you will normally find, are already taken as in our case. We do not like discussing hypothetical situations.

When you want coffee just say so. We do, too (and don't normally get it). 99.9999999% of men are not mind readers – (the rest are idiots.) Incidentally, women too cannot read minds unless you fall into the 0.0000001% category which could be one of the reasons why I still have not got that cup of coffee.

We are good listeners; however we operate better with the TV on high volume with lots of sound and 3D animation effects. It may be worthwhile utilising the tape recorder and letting us listen to your problems at our leisure which would solve all the problems. First, you get to be heard. Second you don't get to listen to any solutions from us. Third we get to watch our cricket match.

With love

From the man in your life

****

I do appreciate his point of view but he is definitely sleeping on the couch tonight!

Hamsters Incorporated

Dealing with loss of any kind is hard. Be it health (sometimes reversible) or a pet (many a time replaceable) or a loved one- never reversible, never replaceable.

A friend mentioned that their pet white rat was dying. It reminded me of our hamsters, in whose company, the children and I had spent many happy hours.

Hamsters are fairly unknown in India. Most people mistake them for rats. Many have not even heard of them and are scared of them. Keeping them as pets is unimaginable.

Originally they were two of them. A male and a female. Chunnu and Munnu. (Yes, they had Indian names.) The children had christened them 'Smartie' and 'Cutie'. But I changed it to Chunnu-Munnu, which I felt was so apt for their cuteness; and it stuck.

They had been bought completely on an impulse. It was my son's birthday the next day, and we were having a nature theme party. We had decided that we would get chicks and it would be fun for the children to hold them and watch them. After the party my maid said she would love to take them away and raise them.

We set out to the pet store wanting to buy chicks. But the hamsters caught our eye. The pet shop owner knew how to charm prospective customers. He put one in his pocket and it peeped out so endearingly with eyes like buttons, resembling Stuart Little. We were completely sold. My son begged and begged for one. I couldn't refuse. After all, it was easier than keeping a dog. So we came back with two hamsters in a cage. My husband was aghast. He never expected it. But now he had no say in the matter any more.

My father-in-law was visiting us for a few days and he was to arrive the next day. The immediate problem on hand was to hide these creatures from him. He does not approve of keeping pets (that too a hamster) and it would mean many hours of listening to his lectures on dangers of it.

I warned the children that if their grandfather came to know of the new pets they would go right back to the store. Now they were accomplices in the crime. My husband too was roped in (He didn't want to listen to the lectures as well!) and when my father-in-law came to stay, we kept the cage in my son's room and shut the door. Whenever my father-in-law tried to go into the room, one of the kids would distract him and take him elsewhere. We managed to keep him out of that room, but it wasn't without close calls.

Meanwhile, the hamsters had let themselves out of the cage. They are very intelligent beings and great escape artistes. It is very difficult to find a hamster as they are tiny and agile. We were also very worried that in case my father-in-law woke up at night and saw them, he would probably kill them, mistaking them for a rat! After a few breathless moments (and since it was still inside the bedroom) we did manage to find both of them, happily hiding inside an old shoe that had been shoved under the cupboard.

Chunnu-Munnu were Syrian golden hamsters. It was great fun to watch how they interacted with each other. The petty fights they had (yes, very much like humans) where the female would then sulk, and the male would go make peace, by offering her either a twig, or sunflower seeds or nuts. Then she would reluctantly agree to accept it. (I am sure secretly she wanted to just run to him, but hey—she should not give in so easily, right?) And in no time they would be 'in action'. Their efforts produced a lovely baby—again very imaginatively christened 'chunnu-munnu baby' by me. (Somehow no other name seemed apt.)

The average lifespan of the hamster is 2 years. Chunnu and Munnu, both died, one after the other. I wish I could tell you that Munnu died of a broken heart—who knows— but scientists and rational thinkers would just attribute it to things like lifespan, and natural ageing process.

We had many good times with Chunnu-munnu baby. We used to watch his antics in delight. He, like his parents, learnt to let himself out of the cage. He could identify me and my son. My daughter was a bit reluctant to handle him, but loved petting him. My husband was fond of him, but terrified and would not even touch him. I remember the time when one of my closest friends, came over to stay. Her children were so at ease with Chunnu-munnu baby. My friend, like my husband, never even touched him.

It was comical (for us) to hear how my husband perfected the art of feeding them when the kids and I went to visit my mom for a few days. He was terrified of opening their cage, and perfected the fine art of dropping sunflower seeds into their bowl through the gap at the top of the cage, his hand positioned very scientifically at a ninety-degree angle which would ensure that they all fell right into the bowl. The hamsters were still alive when we came back and husband's aim had been perfected. If there was a feeding-hamster-without-opening-cage-contest, he would have won it! I guess some people are comfortable with animals and some just are not.

There were ALWAYS a bunch of kids around my son, as they were all fascinated by the hamster.

I sure am glad about the happy memories that we have with chunnu-munnu-baby. Not to mention, it was such a learning process, filled with joy for the kids.

Life in all forms is to be revered and if you manage to do that, you manage to see the magic in life.

****

Some Facts about Hamsters

Hamsters are one of the easiest pets to keep, especially if you live in an apartment. They can be obtained from any reputed pet shop. They are nocturnal creatures. They have cheek pouches that they use to store food. They later bring it out and add it to a stock that they keep, just like squirrels. They don't need to be vaccinated and they do not spread any disease. On the contrary, they can catch a cold from you—therefore it is you who have to be careful about your own hygiene lest the hamster catches an infection from you. The average lifespan of the hamster is about two years and many parents buy a hamster as a pet to teach their children about the joy of caring for another being and also dealing with death and loss.

Life skills Coach for wit and sarcasm

Has it ever happened to you that when someone makes a slightly disparaging remark, you don't know what to say? Hours later when you are thinking about it, a smart repartee strikes you and you wish that you had thought of it right then, at that point of time. It has happened to me sometimes. I think of a clever line, but hours later.

Some people are blessed with quick wit and some I guess train themselves. I don't know which category my mom falls into, but it sure is hard to escape her words that are like a spray from a machine gun, and you are left with multiple holes in your ego, not knowing what to say or do.

Conversations with her always bring me back to the earth with a thud. Sometimes the thud is so softly cushioned that I don't even realize that I have *thud-ed* until the pain slowly shoots up, like the brilliant crimson colours of the sunrise, filling up a piece of drab blue sky.

She has a great sense of humour and ready wit, cleverly clothed in a cloak of sarcasm that unless you are really sharp you don't even realize how her veiled dig just deflated your super puffed up ego as gently as air being let out from one of those travel blow-up pillows. If you aren't used to her, you will most definitely gape with open mouth, like a goldfish in a confined bowl, not knowing what to say. But if you have grown up with her, you become amusingly clever, witty, sarcastic and, at the same time, aggressive in a gentle way, much like those concealed lightings in smart homes that glow without letting you see the source of that candescent light.

Like this one time, when I was a kid, I remember a very pesky guy who used to keep dropping in, uninvited. I could sense that my mom did not like him much. He would make himself very comfortable at any time that was convenient to *him*. Then he would speak about what he did, and where he went and how great he was. He would go on and on. After that (I presume when he ran out of breath) he would keep inviting us over to his home. We never went. After several invitations that never resulted in a visit to his home, he said to my mom in mock frustration, "If the person does not go to the well to drink water, the well has to come to the person." (He was loosely translating a Hindi proverb)

"Oh, that really depends on whether the person is thirsty or not," retorted my mom instantly. It struck home and his unwelcome visits stopped. I remember my dad laughing hard over this.

Another time, we were having an elderly relative visiting us. My mom, in true tradition of Indian hospitality had slaved in the kitchen for hours and had prepared a really delicious, four-course meal, with several accompaniments. This gentleman after hogging like a pig (Not a word in appreciation or a thanks) looked at my brother and me, and made a snide remark asking my mom whether she was feeding us enough, and that we looked like a pair of skeletons.

With an absolutely straight face, my mom replied, "Oh, no. On most days I starve them. But when we have *slightly* gluttonous people over, I let them eat—But only a teeny weenie bit, just in case the food falls short." She smiled sweetly.

He never expected it and I could see the colour draining off his face like a vacuum cleaner sucking up a layer of dust.

I can recall many such incidents.

It is hard to get the better of her. She really has a comic sense of narrating events and, phone conversations with her are always laugh sessions.

She is a great and demanding coach and observing her in action is wonderfully entertaining.

Practice they say makes perfect. In this case it is definitely true.

The promise

"**P**romises should never be broken," says my dad. I always try to keep mine. But today, I made one that I hope I never have to keep.

My dad as a grandfather was every child's dream come true. He was very close to all of us, and especially to my children. My children fondly recall the games that my dad has taught them. My parents lived in a tiny village called Eruveli in Kerala, right next to thousands of rubber tree plantations. Like all small villages there, it is lush green, verdant, peaceful and so unhurried. It is nature at its best. It is picture-perfect.

Any visit to their Grandparents home means hours of endless fun, climbing trees, walking through paddy fields, petting baby goats, eating guavas picked off trees and swimming in the river with my dad. My children were devastated when he died all of a sudden, without any warning or even a hint of things to come, last September He died in the middle of a conversation with mom. Just like that One moment he and mom were watching their favourite show or TV and the next moment he was gone. My mom had initially thought that he has unusually fallen asleep. In a way, he had. Except that from this one, there is no waking up.

My children now know that death can be that way too.

Often, my son (he is 9) and I have these 'mother- son' talks, long after my daughter (she is 6) has drifted off to sleep, after their bed time reading ritual. I don't know if it is the quietness of the night or the intimacy of being cozily curled up in a warm bed, hugging me that reassures him, and he talks to me, so much. He says he loves this time of the day. We talk about many things each night. Last night's conversation brought a lump to my throat, though I managed to hide it well.

"Mommy— how do you think I will die?"

"Hmm—I wish I could answer that but I don't know, Son." I hugged him tighter.

"I wish God made a world where nobody is born and nobody dies and things just stay the same."

"I wish that too. I wish I could just freeze this moment in time. You will still be nine forever and I won't grow older."

"No, Mommy—then I'd have to go to school forever! Who wants to do that? I want to grow up soon, buy a car and take you around."

"Make that a Ferrari. I love Ferraris!"

He was quiet for a minute.

Then he whispers, "I would hate to die without you Mommy."

"I'd hate that too."

"Do you promise that you won't die before me?"

"I promise."

We lay in silence, each of us lost in our own thoughts. That night I held him till he drifted off to sleep.

Free wheelie

It all began when I was about 20. We were staying in Kochi at that time. A cousin of mine who lived in a small town nearby had to board a flight from Kochi. The easiest way for him to reach the airport was by his bike. And since the Airport at that time did not have a facility where he could be assured that his bike was safe for a week (the duration of his trip) he decided to leave it with us. My brother, who was 17 at that time, hesitatingly asked him if we could use it till he came back. My cousin, being a generous soul, readily agreed. (In retrospect I think he was either very trusting or did not care about his bike much or maybe he just did not know how to say no) For my brother and me, it was like manna from heaven. We had a motor-bike all to ourselves for a whole week.

My brother, like most boys his age, knew how to handle it with ease—and he took me for a couple of rides. We felt so great, so grown up and so happy riding around the neighborhood on that bike.

After a couple of rounds, I wasn't content riding pillion anymore and wanted to ride the bike.

"Please show me how to do it," I begged my brother. At first he acted a bit pricey, but after I worked on him a little, (Which consisted of me agreeing to do all his allotted chores for a week, like keeping the garbage out, cleaning the table, taking the dogs out for a walk etc—what is a week after all—I would be learning to ride a bike) he agreed to show me.

The bike had gears that had to be changed with the leg. Whoever has heard of such an absurd concept? At least I hadn't! For cars and for scooters that I could handle with ease, the gears have to be changed with the hand. This one was a new concept for me. Then you have to look forward and accelerate and release the clutch slowly. In theory, I understood it well.

I mounted the bike. I felt great. Visions of those glamorized bike racing champions came to my mind, and I felt so powerful. My brother stood nervously on the side watching me.

"Are you sure you can handle this?" he asked.

"Of course! Don't worry," I said confidently. After all he is younger to me and anything he can do I can do better.

Or so I thought.

I did what he told me to—or at least what I thought he told me to do.

The bike JUMPED, actually jumped into the air four times like a startled toad caught in the headlights of a car at night.

Needless to say, I jumped with it. The sheer fright and shock numbed my senses and I crashed into a banana tree. The bunch of bananas fell down along with the bike and me. And they weren't even ripe!

My parents, my neighbours and even the people who lived behind our house, came running out—and I had to be rescued. To add to my shame, I had to lie there under the bike and the tree, till they lifted the tree first, then the bike. My dad, I think was more concerned that the bananas were uprooted before they were ripe. The shouting that they gave me that day still rings in my ears.

I had to do my brother's chores, too, for a week. After all, a promise is a promise. Neither of us mentioned anything to my cousin when he came back. Fortunately, the only thing damaged in this whole operation was my ego.

That was the end of my trying to learn a bike.

"Oh God, grant me the courage to accept the things I cannot change, to change the things I can and the wisdom to know the difference," goes a prayer.

The older you grow, the more accepting you become. You are willing to be content in the knowledge that there are some things beyond you. Some things that you just can't do. And just because you can't do it, it does not make you inferior in any way.

My ego has accepted it. Or rather, I have brow beaten my ego to accept it, by pacifying it a bit, by repeatedly telling it that I *can* drive a four wheeler, I *can* parallel park with ease and I *can also* drive a two wheeler without a gear and I have great control over a bicycle and I *can even* ride without holding the handle bars.

But when it comes to geared motor bikes, I prefer admiring them— both the bike and the rider. And if the rider happens to be a woman, extra points for her. Wow—here is someone doing something s easily that I just cannot do.

And after all these years, I can say that I have the wisdom to know the difference between trying too hard and accepting.

Mail Exchange

You can pretend it does not exist, you can pretend it isn't there, you can even say it is all a skewed way of looking at it, but the unbiased fact is that it does exist—The gap between the professionally qualified people (The CAs, the IIT-IIMs, the Ivy League graduates) and the lesser mortals (The B.As, the fine arts graduates, Sociologists, Musicians). It is subtle (Okay, sometimes really not so subtle, especially when the financial newspapers scream out the starting salaries being offered to freshers) but there is an underlying patina of smug superiority and intellectual or artistic arrogance that runs deep down among each group.

When I opened my mailbox that morning an email forward caught my eye.

That mail was funny, outrageous but also led me to conclude that only a professionally qualified person could have analysed it that way.

And since my closest friends (including my husband) are professionals (and I am also an artist) there was no way I was taking this lying down.

So I forwarded it to them. And this is what my mail said.

ONLY an Engineer would have looked at it this way. I'm CERTAIN. :)

That's why I like Artists. ;)

Preeti

This was what the forward was:

"I did the math on the Paul McCartney-Heather Mills divorce. After 5 years of marriage, he paid her $49 million.

Assuming they did it every day, once a day, during their brief 5 year relationship (married men all know THAT doesn't happen), it ends up costing him $26,849 per lay, not counting attorney's fees and court costs.

On the other hand, Elliot Spitzer's call girl Kristen charges $4,000 an hour. Crazy, right?

But...

Had Paul McCartney employed Kristen for 5 years he would've paid $7.3 million for an hour of sex every night for 5 years (a savings of $41+million).

Value-added benefits are: a 22 year old hot babe, no begging, no coaxing, never a headache, wide open menu, ability to put BOTH legs around you, no bitching and complaining or "to do" lists. Best of all, she leaves when you're done, and comes back the next day, ready for another round. All at 1/7th the cost, with no legal fees.

Is it just me, or is Kristen a WAY better deal!"

My friend (who is an IIT-IIM graduate) replied back almost immediately. This is what his reply said:

This is great piece of analytical work I must say. Tell me how would have an artist looked at this situation?

This was like giving the mike to a publicity hungry Politician and there was no way I was letting go of an opportunity to voice my very strong feelings suppressed over the years. This is what my reply was:

An artist wouldn't have divorced Heather Mills in the first place. Cost saved: $ 49 million.

He would have wooed Kristen with roses, would have painted pictures inspired by her, would have made her fall in love with him.(which woman can resist such adoration?)

Cost saved:$7.3 million

Then he would have painted beautiful pictures inspired by the love of his life. (Like MF Hussain series dedicated to Madhuri and Renoir painting his lady love and 'Portrait of Adele Bloch-Bauer' by Gustav Klimt – which, incidentally, sold for $135,000,000) Not only has he saved money, he has actually benefited too—emotionally and financially as well.

See—Artists are WAY better than Engineers.

Of course he had to reply back to that. It arrived within 5 minutes.

Artist does not know math or calculations and since he is so engrossed in his work, he would not even know whom he had married and who is the keep. The artist would be so involved that the royalties would actually be going to others' account thus there could be a potential loss in income of 49 Million $ and 7.3 Million $ which anyway those two would have got without working for it. He would be so involved in his work and walking around barefoot that these two would have side business earning them yet another 49 Million $ and 7.3 Million $. Thereby I agree with you that artists are twice as better than engineers as they end up making double the money for these two women!.

Now I had to defend the pride and honour of the entire community of non-professionals (Which anyway, in numbers far exceed the professionals) So I said this:

Artists would EMPLOY engineers/CAs and the likes who will take care of such mundane stuff like accounts for them. (by the way, basic math everyone knows, including artists—but the same can't be said of Art. It requires a certain temperament to *feel* passion and capture it on canvas and even appreciate it)

And as regards knowing who is the wife and who is the keep— how does it matter?!!!

Pat came the reply.....

Surprisingly this mail straight went to junk folder and said it was spam!

By employing accountants and engineers, the loss to the artist is even higher- now even the accountants and engineers get a cut on the royalties and have it for keeps!

This was my reply:

But the artist makes SO MUCH that he doesn't care! What the engineer and CA get are just peanuts—crumbs—miniscule portions—bird feed. You get the picture.

Heh heh.

And see—even the computers of engineers are biased!

To which he said:

Not all artists make SO MUCH, only the barefoot ones do, not the ones who sit around in bungalows... comps were designed by an artist, but to make it work you need an engineer!

I wanted to reply back to that but my computer hung.

Now, that is something which till date had never happened to a canvas and a set of paints.

End of debate. Chapter closed.

The Magic of Faith

It was my daughter's sports day at school. She is 6. A lovely age to be, I think. At least for mothers. You don't have to change diapers; they can talk, they tell you what they want, but most of all they listen to you, adore you and think you are the most beautiful person on Earth and they want to be just like you when they grow up.

It was really sunny and she would have to be standing in the tropical mid-day sun for at least four hours. She wanted to wear a cap. The school she goes to has a prescribed cap. They have prescribed everything, right from school bags to watches to lunch bags to shoes to hair bands to even bloomers, all of which have to be bought at the school tuck shop. You cannot wear any that you like. It has to be the prescribed one. I hadn't bothered to buy a school cap till now, and since she wanted it, I drove her to school that morning, (usually she goes by school bus) so that I could buy the cap and she could wear it for her Sports Day. Through out the way, she kept chattering, excited about the Sports Day and telling me that I was the sweetest mommy on Earth, for agreeing to come to the Tuck shop just to buy her cap. She is a sweet talker and most importantly her eyes shine with honesty, earnestness and enthusiasm—and she is fully convinced and truly believes what she says. She hasn't learnt to lie. (Yet!)

When we reached the Tuck shop, we were in for a disappointment. The guy there said it was 'out of stock'. There were many other parents too going back without a cap. My daughter's face fell. She was so looking forward to the cap that would shield her from the glaring sun.

She looked at me and asked, "Now, what do we do, Mummy? It will be so bright and for four hours I have to stand in the sun." (I don't know if four hours was a figment of imagination but even fifteen minutes is horrible enough—if you have faced the Indian sun you know what I mean.)

I didn't know what to tell her.

"Don't worry," I said, "Today I'll tell the Sun not to shine so hard."

"Can you do that? Will he listen to you?" she asked.

"Of course, he will. Have you ever seen anyone not listening to your mom?"

She smiled and happily ran off to school.

When she came back in the evening, she gave me a big hug.

"Mummy," she said, "The Sun really listened to you. It wasn't so hot, mummy. You are the greatest." I hugged her back.

And just for that moment, I wanted to be six again.

Live Love Laugh

As year after year comes to an end, people all around the world, make their new-year resolutions. Some break it just after a week—some stick to it for as long as three months. And some really determined souls actually succeed in carrying them out. (Yes, there are people like that!)

When last year was coming to an end, I made a list too. Usually I avoid morbid things, but that day I just could not help thinking that we (yes—ALL of us) are one day closer to our death. As each day ticks by, your date with death comes closer. It is funny how death of someone close makes you confront your own mortality. Until then it is something that is far away and something that always happens to other people, never to you.

I decided I would make a list that everybody CAN follow. In fact, not sticking to it would be difficult! When my friends read it, they endorsed it whole heartedly. Many even took print outs of this list and stuck it on their cupboards. At least that is what they told me and I feel happy to believe them.

This is my list:

1. Laugh heartily: Wikipedia defines laughter as 'an audible expression or appearance of merriment or amusement or an inward feeling of joy and pleasure.' It is a proven scientific fact that laughter strengthens our immune system, helps us fight illnesses and reduces problems associated with high blood pressure, strokes, arthritis and ulcers. There are more than 6000 laughter yoga clubs in 60 countries. Some of these laughter clubs that have sprouted across my neighbourhood first shocked me. At first I was startled by the noise. A group of people about 40 in number, all gathered together and laughing like lunatics for no reason was a concept that I had never come across, in the 35 years of my existence. At first I thought it was thunder in the middle of summer season and was flabbergasted. Later when I watched them, I too laughed, because laughter is so infectious.

Humans are the only animals in Nature who can laugh. (Forget the hyenas—what they do is not real laughter.) Research shows that just a few generations ago healthy humans spent 20 minutes a day or more in laughter. But in today's time, laughing time is down to less than five minutes a day in most countries. Everybody loves to have a good laugh. No wonder humour shows and stand-up comedians are flourishing on Television shows. If you have a crazy pal who makes you go into peals of laughter, hold on to that friendship—nurture it, cherish it. It is truly priceless.

2. Have sex often: Who knows what happens after you are dead? Whether there is life after death or not is one mystery science has not been able to solve. For a long time, I completely believed whatever

Brian Weiss had to say. I have read all his books and he is very convincing. But after a while when the effect of the book wore off, I really wasn't so sure anymore.

Maybe, just maybe, we turn into spirits, looking longingly at humans with their physical bodies, still able to touch and feel. So while you are in the physical mode, it doesn't hurt to do it often, provided it is between two consenting adults. (Unless of course you have a medical condition that prevents you from doing it.) Millions of dollars have been spent on research into this topic and studies have concluded that having a vigorous bout burns 200 calories which is equal to jogging 15 minutes on the tread mill. Studies have also concluded that just before orgasm, levels of hormone oxytocin surge to five times their normal level. This releases endorphins (the feel-good hormones) which alleviate pain from all kinds of things ranging from headaches to stress to even migraine. However studies also warn about indulging in casual and unrestrained sex which will only add to stress and guilt, not to mention sexually transmitted diseases and the dreaded disease with no cure—AIDS. So the key is to do it responsibly—and do it often.

3. Spend time with children: The US Department of Health and Human Services conducted a study which measured how people benefited when they spent half an hour or more with children. They suggested that if you do not have kids of your own, volunteer at the local child centre or rely on nieces and nephews or children of friends. They say it helps to awake the inner child in you. If you have your own kids, take time out every day and really pay attention to what *they* want. Most of us are so busy being parents (Get up, Brush your teeth, Do your homework, Hurry or you will be late) that we forget to be a friend. A friend of mine always says, "Don't just present gifts to children. Be present as a gift to them."

If you don't have kids of your own, I'd suggest that you watch them play. Go to a park, relax in an unobtrusive spot and just observe. Be careful just in case an over cautious mom mistakes you to be a paedophile! Spending time with children teaches you so much, apart from amusing and providing a good laugh.

4. Stay away from the grouches and the drains: I have written about radiators and drains. (See the chapter with the same title.) Move away from the drains and seek out the radiators who will bring sunshine into your lives.

5. If you love someone say it: It is really important to enunciate the words. If that is not possible, show it. An unexpected hug can say so much. Miss no opportunity to tell the people who matter that you really love them. If you are shy, send a text. Send an e-card. Send a real card—do whatever it takes, but express it. It will not only make you feel good about yourself, but it will thrill the person who is the object of your affection too. (Provided of course it is reciprocal love.) Nobody can predict what will happen in the next 24 hours. So while you feel it, express it. It may not last forever, but make the most of it while it does.

6. Be content with your body: As long as we are fit and healthy, we should be happy. After all, we aren't going to model for playboy centerfold, a muscle and fitness magazine nor are we going to star in a porn movie. (I presume if you are you will not be reading my book!) The media bombards us with images of men with six pack abs and impossibly thin women. Majority of us have skewed perceptions of an ideal body. This does not mean that one should not strive to lose weight. If one is reasonably fit, one should be happy. A friend was diagnosed with a terminal illness and was given about 3 months to live. She had two children aged 6 and 3. Another friend's husband who had a high flying career passed away at a young age because of a brain tumor, leaving behind his wife and two daughters. Nobody ever thought that something like that could happen to him.

I realized how thankful one has to be if one is healthy, when I was in the hospital with typhoid, fighting for my life. (It was really bad. I was hospitalized for 15 days two years back and after being discharged was on bed-rest for nearly three months) That was an eye opening moment when I realized that even if one does not have a picture perfect body what really matters is to be blessed with the gift of health.

7. **Enjoy the small things**: Look at the sunrise. You are gifted one every single day. Look at the flowers—if there are no flowers, look at the greenery or the waves in the ocean or the blueness of the sky or the placid flowing of the river or the stillness of a lake or the flight of an eagle or even chirping of the insects! Isn't nature marvelous? Take off on a hike. Camp outdoors. Reconnect with nature. One of my favorite activities remains lying in my hammock and gazing at the stars.

Whatever you choose to do live, love and laugh.

How this book came to be

Life has a way of unexpectedly pulling the rug from under your feet. Till it happened to me, I always thought that these are the kind of things that happen to *other* people. These are the kind of things that happen in Bollywood movies. These are the kind of things that you read about and hear about. It can never happen to you.

Yet it did. Healthy people don't drop down dead for no reason. Usually.

But 7th of September 2006 was not a usual day. Well, it seemed like a usual day to start with. My husband was traveling and was in Delhi, which was not unusual. The kids had gone to school, which was very usual. After coming back, they expressed a desire to eat pizza, which was again not very unusual. I agreed to take them to a nearby pizza joint which was slightly unusual. They had a friend playing with them and I took him along as well, after seeking permission from his mom, as it would seem rude to ask him to go home. The kids loved the outing. We were all busy munching pizzas and having a great time, blissfully ignorant and unaware of something that was happening in another part of the world. Something that would shatter my faith in my friends, my outlook towards life, and would change me completely as a person.

We came home and the kid who was playing with my children went to his house. I put the kids to bed early and called up my husband, saying that I was okay, and wanted to sleep early, as I was very tired and asked him not to call me (when he is traveling he usually does—and we chat about our day) and went to bed.

At 10:30 pm the phone rang. It was my husband. He said my dad was dead. I couldn't believe what I was hearing.

"What? What?" I yelled. My brother who was in Mumbai, had been informed and he had called up my husband. They decided that it was best that my husband told me first.

I was in a daze. I did not know what hit me. I think, when something like this happens, we go into a denial mode to cope. My dad's and mom's tickets had been booked to come to Pune (where I had just moved to) at the end of that very month. My brother's wife was expecting their first baby and was 8 months pregnant. My dad had no illnesses which people his age suffer from and not only that, he was also remarkably fit for his age. He had even scheduled meetings for the next day as he was actively involved in many things. Besides, he was just 66—which was not an age that could really be called 'old age'. This just could not be happening.

I had to set out for Kerala (where my parents lived) immediately. My husband managed to arrange for a reliable taxi through his office contacts. There are no direct flights from Pune to Kochi. It was decided that the kids and I would go to my brother's place in Mumbai. My brother's wife, in her advanced stage of pregnancy, could not travel and so it was decided that I would leave my kids with her, and my brother and I would fly to Kerala. My brother managed to get tickets from Mumbai to Kochi by the 5:00 am flight for both of us. My kids, then aged 8 and 5 were very close to my dad. I knew instinctively that it would be too much for them to bear. And I did not want them with me.

It was around 12:30 am, in the middle of the night that the cab arrived. My kids were fast asleep. I asked the cab driver to carry the sleeping children into the cab, one by one. I remember throwing a few clothes into my bag, and packing another bag for the kids, in a complete daze. It takes about three hours for the journey from Pune to Mumbai by road. In between, my kids woke up and asked where we were going. I burst into tears and told them that their grandfather wasn't well and their uncle and I were going to see him. (For the last time—I did not add.) Then I swallowed my tears quickly and pretended to be brave because I did not want to worry them.

I remember being incredibly calm when we arrived at my brother's house. I think we were both in total denial. Two close friends of my brother had arrived and stayed with us that whole night. We were talking about various things and even laughing and joking, as though it was just a normal everyday thing. I think it was our way of coping.

Even on the flight, the gravity of the situation did not hit us. I remember feeling like it was a big adventure. I jokingly told my brother to eat up whatever they gave us on the flight as we would not be able to eat for the next 24 hours. We discussed various relatives whom we had not seen for ages ever since we left Kerala.

Once we arrived, it was a completely different scene altogether. There was a crowd of people waiting outside the picturesque cottage where my parents (now my mom) lived. Everyone was waiting for our arrival. I threw my bag outside and ran to my mom. She hugged me and let out a loud wail. I was stoic and comforted her. My brother had to go and bring my dad's body from the mortuary. He says that moment in time, when they pulled out the body from the freezer and he saw my dad's frozen legs, is something that is etched deep inside him. Dad who was so jovial, loud, positive, inspiring and a towering presence in our lives, was now just a dead body with a number tag attached.

For the next seventeen days my brother and I stayed with my mom. There was a continuous stream of visitors. My dad was the kind of person who would chat up everyone and be completely at ease with everyone—right from the watchman to the head of a Multinational and even ministers and politicians. He had to meet people from all walks of life, in his line of work and always struck a chord with them. Dad always believed in helping others and in fact after retirement had started a Trust and done a lot of Social work, to help the aged who are poor, abandoned or neglected. It is a registered trust called SWAP (Society for Welfare of aged and poor) and is now run by my mom and a close friend of my dad. Dad used to also hold these English conversation classes to teach the village kids to speak English and it was free of cost. People came from all over the country to pay their last respects. Usually, it was dad who did all the talking whenever someone visited. Dad loved to talk, and mom, my brother and I were just shadows. He would carry on the conversation and interact with visitors while we would just sit back and be entertained. My brother and mom are not much of talkers and so naturally the onus was on me to entertain the people who called upon us. I think it was one of the toughest things I have ever done in my life.

On one hand was my grief, my shock, my anger, my pain. All I wanted to do was curl up and be by myself. I was emotionally very close to my dad and my dad adored me. Everything I did was perfect in my dad's eyes. We would speak to each other on the phone almost every day, and even the previous day I had spoken to him. Each thing in that place was reminding me of my dad. I hated it—I wanted to scream. I wanted to die. I wanted to just talk to him once more. I wanted to yell out that this was bloody unfair and I wanted to tell everyone to disappear. I wanted my dad back.

Of course I could not tell all this to the people who came. I could see they were hurting too. Some of them openly wept and told us what my dad meant to them. *I* ended up comforting *them*.

I was on auto pilot. I remember rattling off the sequence of events in the order which they occurred. I was able to completely isolate my emotions and appear stoically calm as I narrated to the visitors, for what seemed to me like the 100th time, the way he died—how he had had his dinner, how he was watching TV with mom, relaxing in his easy chair—and how he suddenly stopped talking. He had closed his eyes and was gone. I could say it all in detail without the slightest trace of regret or pain in my eyes or on my face. Everyone said I was incredibly brave. I had to be. It was the only way I could hide my pain. It was the only way I knew of coping.

We brought my mom back with us. She would stay with my brother till his wife had the baby. I don't think we even bothered about the air tickets that had been earlier booked for mom and dad. Does a person dying count as a no-show passenger? We didn't bother to find out.

After I came back, life for my husband and kids resumed as usual. The kids had their school to go to. My husband had to go to work. I had not yet resumed the workshops on thinking skills that I do for children and I was emotionally in no state to do so. I remember feeling so alone. For days I could not sleep. Each day when I woke up, the first thought that would occur to me was that my dad is no more—and it was like someone had slapped me hard. I would often break down and my kids and husband got very used to it. I didn't feel like going out anywhere, yet, I so badly wanted to talk about it to people.

People don't know how to respond when someone talks about death. There is usually an uncomfortable silence. Most people don't even want to hear. That was a shattering discovery that I made. Till then I had had so many friends— I was jovial, funny, smart and great fun to be with. But when this happened, people were seeing a different side of me for the first time—they saw my tears, they saw my pain—and I was totally broken when I discovered that people who usually talked to me were now avoiding me completely. One friend told me, "I am not ready to talk about this. Please don't tell me anything." I could not believe it. This was a friend I used to chat with, laugh with and have hours of fun, when things were fine. For the first time, I realized what a naïve fool I had been. People wanted me only because I was a source of amusement, an entertainment to them— not because they really cared. For the very first time in my life, I realized that not everyone who laughs with you is a friend.

I remember waking up and functioning like a zombie, sending my kids to school and after my husband left for work, I would log into the Internet, desperately wanting to talk to someone about my pain. Most of my friends said things like 'You will get over it'. 'May his soul rest in peace' and 'At least he did not suffer.' Then they clammed up and suddenly went offline. Laugh and others laugh with you; cry and you cry alone. I was rapidly discovering that this much-used idiom is indeed true.

I was sick of crying in front of my kids and my husband and I began putting up a happy face in front of them. How long can they keep comforting me? My husband was very very supportive and always ready to listen—but I felt bad to think that every day when he came home from work he would only find me in tears. It is not easy to deal with a person who is weepy all the time and who had turned into someone completely opposite of what she used to be.

In a desperate attempt to remain sane, I began painting— a hobby that had taken a back seat for a while. I also started to blog. I joined a social networking site and made new friends. One particular person whom I met online (and whom I have never met in real life) helped me a lot. He had just quit his job and was on his way to join a college in the U.S. He had a couple of months before he joined. He would chat with me for hours. He would call me up and we would talk and talk and talk. I also met an Artist from the UK (whom I later met in real life when I traveled to London) with whom I began exchanging mails. He too had seen pain (he had lost both his parents and a child)—and the mails he used to send felt like he was reading my mind. He understood fully my grief, my anger, my anguish. He gave me strength, as did my other friend. I shall never forget their kindness and I am so grateful that they came into my life at that point of time.

Then I began writing. Apart from the Internet, it found its way to magazines and newspapers. It was cathartic. Little by little I was limping back to life. I now realized how fragile life could be and we really have to GRAB it and live without regrets. I realized the value of being healthy—and the value of having one more day to live.

My feelings are reflected in my writings and lots and lots of people began writing to me saying how my writing had given them hope, how it had changed their outlook and how much it had helped them be positive. Many encouraged me to put it all in a book—and what you are holding in your hands is the result of that.

I hope you enjoy it as much as I enjoyed compiling it.

Live, Love and Laugh. The gift of life is worth cherishing. If you want to do something, do it right now. Don't put it off. If you love someone, tell them, show them, and express what you feel. Live without regrets—and cherish the gift of laughter and life.

Every single moment of it.